native ground

native ground

A NOVEL

phillip h. mcmath

AUGUST HOUSE/*Little Rock*

L. R. ARK.

This publication was made possible in part by a grant
from the National Endowment for the Arts, a federal agency.

First Edition 1985

Manufactured in the United States of America

Library of Congress Cataloging in Publication Data

McMath, Phillip H, 1945-
    Native Ground.

    1. Vietnamese Conflict, 1961-1975--Fiction.
I. Title.
PS3563.C3865N3   1985   813'.54   84-20527
ISBN 0-935304-77-0

Cover design: Prestige Composition of Little Rock
Typography: Photo Type of Little Rock
Book design: Liz Parkhurst
Production artwork: Byron Taylor

for Carol

ACKNOWLEDGMENTS

One day after the war, I drove my motorcycle to a friend's house. We usually spent our time playing chess and talking about books and baseball. That day, however, I brought a short story I had sketched about an offensive that greeted me my first week "in-country." (Henry Kissinger mentions this offensive on page 282 of his book *White House Years*. From this enemy action he draws the inference that the North Vietnamese were not men of "good will.") This was nothing more than a torso of a short story but I, nevertheless, wanted Steve Chapman's opinion. Steve and I had been friends before the war, and now I was back in Fayetteville, Arkansas to study law; he had never left, once telling me that his living in Fayetteville was one of the "few absolutes of the twentieth century." He took the writing without much comment and proceeded to beat me in chess, even though I had the white pieces.

A few days later, I returned for another game and was confronted with what was obviously my typing paper, spread open over the board. I sat down. He smiled slightly, blowing smoke over his black beard, then told me that he had looked at my "stuff" and that he thought it had some potential but that it needed a framework. A more detailed discussion ensued, followed by another game of chess, the result of which I have frankly forgotten. Steve knows books. All I wanted was his hint to go on.

The book is about, among a lot of other things, time and fate. Today, we hear fate referred to in the context of "environmental factors" or "circumstances." I think the Greek idea is better. It was Christopher's fate to go to Vietnam, just as it was mine. He could not have helped going there anymore than I, once given a nudge, could have helped writing this book. The framework was always there waiting for the command, like a pawn initiating a gambit that carries its own force and direction.

Though Christopher and I shared similar fates, the novel is not autobiographical, it is fiction. Real people will be searched for in vain, and real events are not to be found. I think many good works of fiction have a certain dream-like quality, and I have attempted to create this feeling here.

I have shown the manuscript in its various stages to people whose opinions I value. Clark Closser, Rosemary Henenberg, the late Ben Kimpel, and Chuck Woodard are all friends and scholars who gave me invaluable suggestions and encouragement. I owe them a great deal.

Additionally, I am indebted to Ted and Liz Parkhurst of August House for their publishing efforts and editing assistance. The service they are rendering for the people of Arkansas and Arkansas writers is immeasurable.

Likewise, I would like to thank my marvelous secretary, Frau Christa Sueppmayer Black, who with good German diligence and efficiency suffered through innumerable rewrites without complaint.

More importantly, I acknowledge the love, support and patience of my wife, Carol, who supported me in this effort from its inception. I have dedicated this book to her.

P.H.M.

GLOSSARY

ACTUAL: *Any commanding officer; used in radio traffic to draw distinction between the Commanding Officer and the radio operator.*

AK-47: *An automatic assault rifle used by Viet Cong and NVA forces.*

AO DAI: *A colorful woman's dress worn by Vietnamese on special occasions.*

ARTY: *Artillery.*

ARVN: *Army of the Republic of Vietnam; can be used in the singular or collectively; not noted for their military prowess.*

B-40: *A light, hand-held rocket, used by the Viet Cong and North Vietnamese soldiers against tanks and enemy personnel.*

BAC BAC: *To kill or shoot in Vietnamese.*

BASKETBALL: *A large illumination flare usually dropped from aircraft.*

BODACIOUS: *Marine slang for anything large or bigger than normal, or great many.*

BOO-COO: *A bastardization of the French word "beaucoup" meaning more than normal, or great many.*

BOUNCING BETTY: *An American made anti-personnel mine that, once stepped on, bounced to about waist high before exploding.*

BRONCO: *A small observation aircraft used for the adjustment of air strikes and artillery fire.*

BROWN BAR: *A Marine Second Lieutenant; usually a Platoon Commander with the reputation for having experienced a high percentage of casualties in Vietnam.*

BUSTING CAPS: *To shoot up a lot of ammunition, or to fire upon the enemy.*

BUTTON UP: *A Marine armor term meaning to close all the hatches on a tank.*

BUY THE FARM: *A Marine slang term for one infantry unit having its position overrun by another enemy infantry unit.*

CAC: *Civic action cadre; a small Marine unit assigned to a particular village or villages for the purposes of pacification.*

CANISTER: *A tank round, rather like a shotgun, shooting large pellets and used against infantry.*

CHAO BA: *A Vietnamese expression for "Hello" when addressing a married female.*

CHAO ONG: *A Vietnamese expression for "Hello" when addressing an older man.*

CHARLIE: *Marine slang for the Viet Cong.*

CHOPPER: *Helicopter.*

CO: *Commanding Officer.*

COC: *Command Operation Center; the Headquarters for a battalion or larger unit, usually in a bunker.*

CORPSMAN: *A Navy medic attached to Marine forces; generally suffering a high percentage of casualties and held in high regard by all Marines.*

DIDI: *Vietnamese word for "to leave quickly" or to "run off."*

DINGED: *Marine slang for being killed or wounded.*

FIRE-FOR-EFFECT: *To mass artillery fire on a particular target for the purpose of destroying same; to be contracted with firing a small number of rounds for adjustment purposes.*

FO: *Forward observer; someone who adjusts artillery or mortar fire.*

FREQ: *Radio frequency.*

GET SOME: *Marine slang for engaging the enemy in an aggresive way.*

GOOK: *An American word referring to any person of oriental extraction; sometimes referred to as "Gooner" or "Luke-the-Gook;" the latter phrase being reserved particularly for the enemy.*

GREEN MACHINE: *Marine slang for USMC.*

GREEN WEENIE: *A raw deal, usually at the hands of the Marine Corps.*

GRUNT: *Any Marine infantryman regardless of rank.*

GYPSY RACK: *A small cage-like device welded to the back of a turret of a tank for the purposes of carrying personal gear, miscellaneous equipment, and important items like beer, cokes and c-rats.*

HAM-AND-MOTHERS: *A slang word used by Marines to designate ham and eggs, which is a brand of c-ration or canned food which was the usual fare for all Marine units when hot chow was not available.*

HE: *High explosives to be distinguished from other types of artillery, mortar, and tank rounds such as willy peter (white phosphorous) and canisters, etc., almost always used when firing for effect.*

HONCHO: *The man in charge.*

HOOCH: *Any shanty or hut lived in by Marines or Vietnamese.*

HOUSE MOUSE: *A female Vietnamese house servant.*

ILLUM: *Short for illumination flare which could be fired by aircraft, artillery, mortars, or, in the smaller variety, by infantry.*

JOHN WAYNE: *A verb or adjective meaning to be flashy, take short cuts, be overly daring, etc. It was sometimes said that there were two ways of doing anything in the Marine Corps, "the right way" or the "John Wayne way."*

KIA: *Killed in action.*

LAYING PIPE: *Sexual intercourse. Sometimes called "leg" or "legging" (noun and verb).*

M-16: *A standard American assault rifle developed as a counterpoint to the Communist AK-47.*

M-60: *A standard American machine gun carried by infantry units.*

M-79: *A hand-held infantry grenade launcher sometimes referred to as a "blooper." The weapon looked like a large shotgun and was able to shoot grenade-like projectiles farther than could be thrown by hand.*

M-106: *A crew-served recoilless rifle originally designed for anti-tank purposes, but used in Vietnam as a defensive weapon against infantry.*

MAMA SAN: *A Vietnamese female civilian, usually elderly. Also Papa San and Baby San.*

MEDEVAC: *Medical evacuation, usually by "chopper."*

NUMBER ONE: *The best.*

NUMBER TEN: *The worst.*

NVA: *North Vietnamese Army which was to be distinguished from those guerilla forces from the South referred to as "VC" or "Viet Cong."*

OP: *Outpost; a forward position used for patrolling and reconnaissance.*

POP-UP: *A small, hand-held illumination device rather like a roman candle used to illuminate one's immediate front when nothing else was available.*

R&R: *A particular unit or groups of units sent to relieve one beleaguered by enemy action.*

RPG: *Rocket propelled grenade; a hand-held anti-tank weapon used by the Viet Cong and North Vietnamese against American tanks; generally considered quite effective and greatly respected by tankers.*

RICKY-TICK: *To do something in a hurry.*

ROUND-EYE: *Any occidental female.*

S-3: *The Operation and Training Officer of a battalion or regimental staff. On the battalion level this rank is held by a Major, and in Vietnam he was responsible to the Commanding Officer of the battalion (a Lieutenant Colonel) for the tactical deployment of the battalion; depending on personalities, this position was often times in importance second only to the Commanding Officer.*

SHIT TOGETHER: *Marine slang for any unit or individual that was proficient; sometimes referred to as having one's "shit in one bag," as opposed to having one's "shit scattered." It was generally believed that the VC and NVA had their "shit together," whereas the ARVNS' "shit was scattered."*

SITREP: *Situation report.*

SKATE: *The doing of something with little or no difficulty.*

SKINNY: *Any news, sometimes referred to as the "hot skinny," or the "hot cock."*

SKIPPER: *Slang for a Marine officer in command of a company but sometimes used in reference to the Commander of a reinforced platoon or large outpost.*

SKY OUT: *To retreat or run off quickly.*

SNUFFY: *Any Marine enlisted man, usually of a lower rank.*

SWEEP: *To look for mines on a road or a particular area, usually done by engineers. In another context, it can also mean to send a unit through an area looking for the enemy.*

TANKER: *A Marine term for personnel assigned to tank units, equivalent to armor in the Army. In the Marine Corps each division is supported by one tank battalion. However, unlike the Army, Marine tanks are rarely employed in large units but are generally assigned to support the infantry in smaller groups of twos, threes and fives.*

UTILITIES: *Technical Marine for green or camouflaged dungarees.*

V.C.: *Viet Cong; any Vietnamese Communist guerilla fighting against American and South Vietnamese forces, used to distinguish the indigenous Southern guerillas from the regular NVA army units.*

VILLE: *Village.*

WIA: *Wounded in action.*

WILLY PETER: *A white phosphorous marking round sometimes referred to as smoke; used by artillery, tanks and mortars for the purposes of marking and adjusting fire, or, for the alternate purpose of blinding the enemy.*

THE WORLD: *Home.*

YIE YAE: *A lecher.*

ZAPPED: *To be killed.*

I went to the dresser and took up the watch, with the face still down. I tapped the crystal on the corner of the dresser and caught the fragments of glass in my hand and put them into the ashtray and twisted the hands off and put them in the tray. The watch ticked on.

Faulkner, *The Sound and the Fury*

1

THE RAIN HAD ALMOST stopped when First Lieutenant Shaw looked out of his bunker into the Vietnam night. There was fighting on the mountain in front of him. Quickly, red tracers sped across the valley striking the hillside before ricochetting into the darkness. He lifted his binoculars focusing on the battlefield illuminated by phosphorous flares drifting under silk parachutes. Now he could see mortar rounds burst on the hillside, coverging with the machine gun fire in quick explosions.

Christopher watched casually for a time, but all he could make out were more tracers and mortar fire, dim in the aurora of flare light.

North Vietnamese, he thought, still focusing.

Now and again a muzzle flash would answer from the other side of the valley, but that was the only sign of the enemy.

Despite the fighting, the morning remained still along his Battalion's immediate front; for some reason, "Charlie" had chosen to leave them alone and attack Fox Company. Christopher lowered his binoculars and lighted a cigarette, watching the smoke drift upwards highlighted by the flares floating like specters over the silver barbed wire. A flare hissed out, falling with a clanking sound behind him. There was muffled laughter in the trenches nearby, oblivious to the action on the mountain.

The field phone rattled next to his arm.

"Shaw here," he said, picking up the receiver.

"How's it look?" came the voice on the other end. It was Captain Stoner, the Battalion's assistant operations officer.

"Fox is in to it."

"How bad?"

"Bad enough."

"Regiment still hasn't come up with a report or anything. Still sorting things out I guess. You know, hoping like hell it's a probe or something."

"It's not a probe."

"What is it?"

"Well, you know how they've been talking about a big offensive."

"You think this is it, Chris?"

"It's something."

"Yeah, I agree; it's happening all over."

"Some tours gonna end today, Captain."

"Colonel Zell is nervous; this stuff makes him real uptight."

"There's reason to be nervous."

"How is Fox doing? We've got em on the horn and they seem to have things under control."

"They're doing all right. Looks like they caught em in the wire."

More machine gun fire erupted in frantic bursts.

"Good. That's what they've been telling us; caught em in the wire. Maybe things'll settle down with first light. We've ordered up some more illumination from Regiment, they'll have it flying over later kicking out basketball flares. Our mortar illum is getting kinda low."

"It's all lit up now, our night vision is shot."

"We'll just have to keep it up until morning. What are the gooks using?"

"The usual; mortars, small arms but no B-40 rockets yet. No doubt they got em stuffed away somewhere. Seems like they're all dug in real good, probably in tunnels and holes."

"We'll never find em all; they'll vanish with the sun."

"Maybe. Seems like they mean business, Captain, they may stay awhile this time."

"I hope not."

"This is going on all over the Division, right?"

"Yeah, everywhere, the whole area sounds like Dodge City."

"War is our business, right?"

"Don't start that, Shaw."

"Who's assigned to React with my tanks?"

"Lieutenant Malone, Echo Company."

"I thought Andy was skating in the rear these days."

"Got his ole platoon back since Boswell got blown away."

"How's Boswell doing?"

"He's not, Zell got the word about midnight."

"Bad?"

"Sorry, Shaw."

"Goddamn."

"I know, man. I'm sorry."

"Boswell was okay."

"It's bad, but he was all fucked up, probably better off."

"I heard it was a mine."

"That's the report. A Bouncing Betty."

"We give em to the ARVN and they give em to the gooks."

"Then we get em back again. Crazy, ain't it?"

"Real goddamn crazy."

"Radio operator had this nutty idea about stepping off the trail to take a piss and zappo. Killed him, of course, but I thought Boswell might pull through.

Happy Valley is bad news. He had a little John Wayne in him but Boswell was gonna be a good one. He just needed more time in the bush. I think he wanted to stay in the Corps."

"That's what he told me."

"It's hard to outthink a goddamn mine. We tell em not to bunch up, but it ain't enough. The damn things are everywhere. Maybe we can even things up today, Chris."

"So Malone is back in the war? I know he's happy about that, short as he is. He's bound for the 'Freedom Bird' real soon."

"Yeah, gets to be a platoon leader again, hero for a day, till another rosy cheeked kid comes down the pipe. I tell you Zell is glad for the excuse to put him back in the field; he figures he's our best Grunt Lieutenant anyway. Echo Company has been skating a lot, not doing much, so we're using them for the React, if there is one. You know, give em something to do."

"I'm sure they really appreciate the favor, Captain."

"Zell really don't want to send the React out if he can help it, but he may have to; Regiment'll demand it. You know how they are; think we ought to still try and win the war."

"Those guys have funny ideas."

"It's the investigations that bend him out of shape."

"Those investigations really getcha down, don't they?"

"Look Shaw, he just don't want to get shit on this late in the tour. He's up for full Bird and he don't want it blown now because of some goddamn gook offensive."

"I can't come up with any sympathy."

"You don't have to, nobody expects it. I'm just trying to explain the crazy bastard to you."

"Zell I understand; it's Craig I can't figure."

"He's hard-core."

"And more."

"Look, Shaw, just let us know if things get any hotter; we're trying to keep our finger on this thing, okay?"

"Sure."

"I'll be here until Major Craig relieves me."

"Fine."

"And I'll let you know if anything firms up on your React."

"Thanks."

"Right."

Jesus, said Christopher to himself, hanging up the receiver and flipping the cigarette toward the wire. *In country just two months, and zap.* Boswell was a twenty-two-year old from Texas, "from the valley," he had said, "good farm country," and in a hurry to become a Marine Second Lieutenant.

Captain Stoner had radioed yesterday with the news. Boswell had been medevaced to the hospital ship *Repose* in Da Nang harbor, but Christopher had not been optimistic. He was never optimistic about a mine.

Christopher thought, *Boswell's platoon must have run right into the lead elements of this bunch now fighting Fox. Things have been quiet for weeks, then suddenly all sorts of shit starts. Then Boswell's replacement got into it. That should have been a tip off. This is a big outfit, and it's here to stay.*

Mortar fire fell on the far hillside in another wave of thudding explosions.

One of Christopher's tanks, sitting behind the wire, started its engine, idled for a minute, then moved to another position. Christopher was pleased; he had told them to move at night so that they would not be targeted by RPG anti-tank rockets.

His thoughts quickly returned to his dead friend. *He just needed a little more time, then he would have been pulled back and replaced; then he would have made it.*

Christopher stared aimlessly at the fighting for a time, then took off his helmet, sat down, and tried to sleep. It was nearly five o'clock in the morning and the rain had stopped. It was December and he wished he were home.

2

"WAKE UP, CHRISTOPHER, wake up," said Conrad, leaning over the bed.

Christopher opened his eyes and look up at his father. He did not stir, but simply peered into his father's blue eyes. Conrad was tall, athletic, with sandy hair. To Christopher he seemed a giant, omnipotent, almost flawless.

"Wake up, Son, we need to get going."

It was light in the room. It had been dark. Christopher preferred the dark. He turned his head toward the bedroom window. It was still black outside. He wished now he had not told his father that he wanted to go on the hunt this morning. All he wanted was to go back to sleep. It was early December, the woods would be cold, and today it all seemed silly to wake up before one had to and go into the forest.

The brightness hurt his eyes and he turned his face downward into the pillow to escape the lighted room. What had been warm and secure had changed into an unpleasant reality, and he buried his face into the sheets.

"Come on, Son. Get up. Get up. We need to get a move on."

"Yes, sir," he mumbled.

"Get up. Let's go."

"I'm up. I'm awake now."

"Up, up."

"Yes, sir." He rolled over shielding his eyes with his forearm.

"You need to get out of bed. Mother'll have breakfast finished soon."

Christopher threw aside his blanket as if it were a heavy weight and got reluctantly out of bed.

"Your shotgun is already in the truck. All you need is to get dressed and come on down and eat. We need to leave right away; we need to get a good start."

"Yes, sir."

"They'll be turning the dogs loose soon."

"Okay," mumbled Christopher as he slowly searched for his clothes in the dresser by the bed.

"Dress warm."

"Yes, sir," he repeated, putting on his clothes mechanically.

The "long-handled" underwear was tight and the bottoms had to be stretched and pulled up to the hips for a snug fit. He wiggled into the tops, tucking them into the elastic of the waistband. Out of the closet he found his favorite plaid shirt that resembled the one he had seen a man wearing in an outdoor magazine. The man had been sitting by a fire near a Canadian-looking lake with his tent in the background. Christopher loved these magazines and saved them by the stacks. He especially liked a writer named Ruark who wrote in serials for one of them. He had always wanted a safari hat like Ruark's with a floppy bill and leopard skin around the base of the crown. Christopher reached into the top of the closet and got out his red baseball cap; people were supposed to wear red hunting in Arkansas.

"Someday I'll have a hat like Robert Ruark," he said, looking at himself in the mirror with the cap cocked on his head. He tugged at the bill and adjusted it over his eyes.

After putting on a pair of jeans, and lacing his leather boots over two pairs of socks, he folded a sweater and brown hunting coat under his arm and started down the stairs for breakfast.

Conrad had already descended the stairs of his large, two-storied house built a few years after the war. He had insisted that it be done in the grand Southern style with Corinthian columns and a long, tree-lined drive circling up to the imposing white facade. "Imitation ante-bellum," Elizabeth Shaw quipped when she first saw the plans he had sketched on the dining table in their old home. The "Ole Place," as it was called, had been quite simple, ranch-style with one story, and had provided shelter for them during the early days of struggle, but it had to be torn down to make room for Conrad's dream. After a time, he had decided that the front was "only for looks," because the part of the house he loved was the kitchen across the back with its large fireplace and wide windows looking out over his fields.

"You get him up?" asked Elizabeth from the stove where she was cooking.

"Well, I think so. Seems like he's having second thoughts when it comes to gettin up on a cold morning, instead of just talking."

"Could hardly get him into bed last night for looking forward to it," she added busily, turning the bacon in the skillet.

"He'll be down, all heavy-eyed," Conrad said as he gazed out of the large window into the blackness as he had done many times. For some reason, he imagined it was the hunt, he thought of his dead father and mother, and of his brothers and sisters. Conrad Shaw had become a big man in the Arkansas Delta, first in farming, then politics. He had been elected to the State Senate for three terms. But is was of his family that the thought: defeated, both the living and the dead, defeated by those same fields that had made him rich, defeated by the little white plant that made the fingers sore and the back ache, that tried to pull you out of school, such as it was, until you had to run away, or be beaten, as he had done one desperate night, fleeing to the University in the hills. He would never forget them or the terrible labor: the bending, pulling, grasping, stuffing over and over endlessly. King Cotton was a tyrant all right, and he had no mercy. Conrad stared at his fields lying peacefully in the morning mist, and he thought of those poor ghosts strangled in youth with whatever spark they may have had stillborn inside them. He had just awakened his only son, and he now remembered when his father had awakened him countless times to another day of drudgery in the fields. "Poor ones," he thought almost out loud as he waited for Christopher to come down and the hunt to begin. "Poor ones," he whispered again to the fields that shrouded his memories in a dark morning fog.

He took another sip of coffee. Politics, like war, had been intoxicating. After both were over Conrad suffered a sense of emptiness not alleviated by the success of the farm. Had he made a mistake, taken a wrong turn? No, he concluded time after time; he had been lucky.

Now the mist seemed to lift a little in anticipation of the sun, the ploughed earth surfacing into view.

Later, after he had done well, his mother had been proud of him for running away and eventually going to college, even though he had left the family short-handed. He wished that she had lived longer. He wished both of his parents had been able to see him vindicated. Pappy had died while Conrad was in Europe, shortly after Normandy, when Major Shaw was busy winning medals in the hedgerow country. If it had to happen, he was secretly glad it had happened that way; Pappy was worn out, and Conrad hated funerals. It seemed for the best, especially with so many young men dying around him, the death of an old man was less unfair somehow. Mother's death was more difficult, he thought, more painful, different, lasting as it did for weeks upon weeks. She had come from the Mississippi hill country to be married here but always wanted to go back. After Pappy died and her children had gone, she went back to Mississippi. She had nothing to hold her so she just left, and Conrad had no choice but to travel back and forth. She had said she "…wanted to be near her people at the homeplace and be able to go to her church near the family plot and be buried there when the time comes." The family plot was poorly kept, grown up in briars near a pine thicket, not far from the "homeplace" which was a little shack returning to the earth like everything seems to do eventually in the South, nothing really changing, just seeming to change, gradually being drawn down into the bowels of time and oblivion like Mother wanting to go back home to Mississippi to die, back to the same kind of clay and mud that had made them slaves in the first place. It was strange, just like Conrad coming home after the war when he didn't really have to, but coming anyway, out of guilt, he guessed, and pride too, knowing that this was the last chance to escape it all, but coming back to the Delta because Mother was old, he said to himself, and needing help and being hurt if he hadn't come back, always fearing for his soul; all she ever wanted was to hold the family together and save their souls. The saving-of-souls, that was most important of all. So Conrad got on the train and headed back South coming to Arkansas like it was the first time since running away that night, being inexorably pulled homeward knowing that it was impossible to do anything else, but vowing to build an empire as compensation, to "show em," which he had done and now was bored with.

21

The mist seemed to lighten even more. The coffee was cold, so he set it on the window sill.

Pappy's family never gave a damn about where they were buried or what happened afterwards, just wanting to keep moving west looking for good cheap land; first North Carolina, Alabama, then Arkansas, where Pappy stopped because he liked the soil, with the rest moving on to Oklahoma and Texas where they lost touch. All they ever really had was a thirst for land, dedication to work, and mistrust of outsiders and Yankees. Always broke and ignorant, wanting vaguely to leave the South, but mistrusting anything that wasn't Southern, and taking it with them until it rubbed off finally somewhere out West. Pappy stayed behind stubbornly holding on to his crazy idea about this soil being the best anywhere, which it was, but not understanding that it wasn't cheap anymore. He died broke.

Elizabeth set the table.

Mother was a saint, he thought. *Not caring much about money unlike Pappy who thought of nothing else, just our souls. She wanted something else better all right, but had no idea how to give it to us, and not really knowing what "it" was, and a little afraid of it since it might destroy our faith, and faith held things together, gave life meaning and purpose despite all the hardships and bitterness. In the end it was faith that made her want to go back to Mississippi to die and be buried in an insignificant pine thicket choked with briars and weeds like it was some holy place or sacred ground instead of old red mud on which men broke their backs trying to farm.*

Conrad had lost his faith, a fact he concealed from his mother and now tried to hide from Elizabeth since she was devout and wanted to raise Christopher the same way. "More precious than gold," his mother had said.

A sleepy figure of a boy entered the kitchen with a sweater and a hunting coat draped over his arm and a red baseball cap cocked arrogantly over one drowsy eye.

"Would you like some coffee, Son?" his mother asked quietly. "Sure he would," said Conrad. "You know he loves his coffee in the morning." Christopher was now allowed to drink coffee and own a gun since he had just celebrated his twelfth birthday. As his mother brought him a cup of black coffee, Christopher moved in front of the large brick fireplace where a fire was kept going on cold mornings. He enjoyed the fireplace and was fond of warming by it each day before breakfast, and now, dreading to leave it for the cold of the hunt, it suddenly seemed strange to him that men would leave the warmth of their home for the frozen woods when they did not really have to. Odd, he thought, that men should desire this. However, as the back of his legs scorched and the coffee opened his eyes, Christopher felt the irresistible urge to hunt with his father grow stronger until it overcame his desire to remain in his mother's kitchen.

"We're running late. Just grab something and let's go," said Conrad after a glance at his watch.

"Here's some toast and bacon," said Elizabeth. While she spoke, she quickly placed the food on a napkin and forced it into her son's hands as he moved toward the door.

"What time do you think you might get back?" she asked, running her hand through her straight black hair.

"'Bout eleven," answered Conrad as he put on his tattered, patched hunting coat and reached for his Stetson hat perched on the gun rack by the back door. His .30/.06 was already hanging in the back window of his pick-up truck.

"Be careful."

"He'll be with me."

"I know."

"Let's go, Dad."

"Goodbye," she said, standing tiptoe waiting for Conrad's kiss.

"Goodbye, dear."

"I'll have lunch ready."

"Fine, we'll sure be hungry."

"Bye, Mom," said Christopher, trying to avoid his mother's affection.

"Have fun, dear," she replied as she touched Christopher with her lips and tugged at the throat of his coat and sweater in an effort to keep in the warmth of the kitchen.

"Let's go, Son," urged Conrad as he walked outside, got into the truck and started the engine.

Elizabeth quickly closed the door against the cold air that rushed into her home. As she looked out the door's small window, she saw the truck lights bounce in a quick, half-circle before disappearing into the oblivion of the dying night.

3

IT WAS QUIET IN the kitchen as Elizabeth sat looking into the flame with black coffee smoke rising in soft curls above her sturdy hands. As the oak log burned, she reflected that fall in the Delta was quite different from the solitary Ozark hills of her youth. There the mountains turned first to fall-reds and yellows then smoky-winter-blue and back again to lush, steamy green. In the Delta, things were flat; there were no secret waterfalls that a child might pretend to discover; no brooks to follow in the forest, appearing, bending and disappearing mysteriously again among the rocks and trees. Only a few surviving stands of hardwood timber stood on the level farm country lying like a great grey scar escorting the Mississippi on its way to the sea. In unbroken fertility the land remained; heavy, monotonous, drained by somber sloughs, backwaters, and small swamps that moved almost imperceptibly on their way to swollen, muddy rivers that accepted them without comment, like time itself.

Elizabeth sipped the coffee and brushed back her hair as her blue eyes fell upon the face of Conrad's father, Pappy, enshrined over the stone mantel. *Strange*, she thought. It was nothing more than a fading black-and-white photograph that was turning brown about the edges, yet there he stood, eyes staring sadly out, shaded only by the visor of a ruined grey Stetson, with his hands hanging down by his side in a gesture of surrender, and resignation.

"Like Hamlet's ghost," Christopher would observe in later years when he returned home from college and had drunk too much on Christmas Eve.

"List, list, oh, list, if thou didst ever thy dear father love," he said too dramatically with the fire flickering on his face, flushed as it was with whiskey.

"List, oh list," repeated Christopher, making everybody stir. "To a son he speaks," he quoted again, "the son of his soul."

Elizabeth stood and turned her back to the flame to warm her housecoat.

"I remember the first day I met your father," she would tell Christopher that same philosophical night. "We had just arrived on the train, and he and a lot of upperclassmen had come down from 'the hill' to check out that year's crop of freshmen women. We weren't to be referred to as 'girls'; it was the 'Women's Dorms,' 'Dean of Women,' and so on. It was the same with the men. It was not until the war that we became 'boys' and 'girls' again, forever to remain so, too. The boys went to war, and the girls stayed faithfully behind, rationing gas and tending to victory gardens. I have to confess I enjoyed the war thoroughly. I know that's an awful thing to say, but it was a great adventure for us all. In a sense, it was a way out; it uprooted us in a manner that we secretly wished for, never again to be the same. Even if we did come home, it wasn't ever to be quite the same again. We were permanently changed."

"For the better?" Christopher would ask, forgetting Hamlet for the moment.

"Yes, for the better. At least I was. Oh, I know it's terrible, men were destroyed by the war and people suffered horribly, but for my generation at least, we learned by it and became broader people. The old paradox about gaining insight through suffering, I guess. We grew through our sacrifice."

"Fortress America was a help," Christopher would add.

"I don't know what you mean."

"Well, it was a luxury, having the war perform some sort of consciousness expansion trick for you, complete with swing music and all."

"You don't understand."

"I think I do understand, more than you think."

"Not really."

"Mom, America went to war with violin music in the background while everybody else was hearing bombs."

That was to come, but this morning Elizabeth thought about Conrad's father and how he had bequeathed nothing to him but his tired dream that Conrad had fulfilled without it being his own; just thinking it was and not really knowing his own, merely living out Pappy's without understanding and feeling vaguely unhappy about it, but doing it anyway out of some stubborn sense of pride and guilt and duty, and because he had to come back home to take care of his mother (and would have anyway) but not wanting to come back, just returning and working, and building, and becoming a big landowner like Pappy wanted for himself, until he realized after it had been done that it wasn't enough, hungering for something that he could not buy or satisfy, longing for something the world could not or would not provide; happy yet unhappy, making even more money, buying even more land, running for the legislature, accumulating more success with an uncanny gift for farming and the land, and men, and wealth, still wanting more, wanting something else but not saying, just letting her realize his unhappiness, feeling he had made a wrong turn and trying endlessly to sort it out staring out the window vacantly at some of the richest fields in the Delta, figuring it must have been when he came home to take care of his sick mother after the war with Pappy dead, driven back here to Arkansas because he left them one night when they were short-handed and needed him: *Money is a curse,* she thought, *I could go back to the hills and live modestly I guess, but he won't, it's too much to give up now and it would take a saint to do that; besides, he still doesn't know what he would do if he did, or what it is he really wants.*

There was a noise near the back door as Queeny came bustling into the kitchen wrapped in a heavily patched coat.

"Morning, Queeny," smiled Elizabeth.

"Morning, Ma'am. They eat?" she asked, busying herself automatically in front of the sink where dirty dishes and pans were piled and waiting.

"You know Conrad, up with the fire roaring by four, never seems to sleep, and Christopher, we had to drag from bed and feed on the way out."

"Huh," grunted Queeny, "I sho don't know why they wants to go out in that col woods fur if'n they don't have to. I nearly froze to def comin over her this mornin, sho did, an that Barrel jes like em, he gone too, tween chors, course, but he be der this e'ning. He jes itchin, sho is, jes itchin to getta loose into them woods and stay there ever extra minute he got. Like that when I married em though, can't be complaining none, cause I knowed that when I started out wid em, sho did."

"It's in the blood, I'm afraid, Queeny."

"Yessum, sho is, like a fever. An there ain't no curin it neither, no way. It's there for good, mineswell forget bout that."

"They'll sure be hungry for lunch; we better get ready."

"That's fo sho, they will be that. It awful ain't it, they jes alike, white and black, when it come to this here fall-fever, that's what I calls it, fall-fever. It sure get a holt of em. In stock, rabbits and hogs, it leave out when the firs fros come, but with men-folk it come sho as the world when that firs fros hit the groun, sho does, an grabs em good too."

"Work and hunting, that's all they think about Queeny, just like my dad and brothers, working and hunting, one or the other. We'll be practically widows from now on Queeny."

"Well, that's right, Miss Lizabeth, widows till spring, an there ain't no hep'n it neither. I is all alone now with my William in the Army and my Sadie teaching school. I won't see hide n'hair of Barrel while he's a huntin, then when that's th' ough, he'll be workin again. Sho will. There just ain't no fixen it, sho ain't. Might as well get used to that."

Maybe he should have stayed in the Army, he was happiest there, thought Elizabeth, drinking her coffee empty.

The four white columns of the Shaws' house had faded away before Christopher noticed a tinge of light in the eastern sky. They traveled in silence down a gravel road that ran along Conrad's fields. Conrad drove to another road that turned sharply to the left, which then took them to the edge of a large cottonfield that lay in barren anticipation of winter.

"Will there be many dogs today, Dad?" asked Christopher, after a while.

"Should be. McPhail has his camp just behind our back gate," replied Conrad, referring to a neighboring farmer who always hunted near Conrad's timber land, bordering as it did on the Bayou Blanc Wildlife Refuge. Conrad shifted into a lower gear as the road degenerated into mud with deep ruts cut into the nearly frozen earth. "He'll have plenty," he concluded, as he concentrated on keeping the truck in the muddy tracks. "Always does," he

26

added, holding the wheel straight.

Christopher, unconcerned with the mire of the road, lapsed into thought as he looked into darkness. He tried to imagine events of the morning; would they be successful; would they even see anything; would his father let him shoot or take the shot himself with his .30/.06 rifle? He finished the remainder of the food his mother had given him and put the stained napkin in the pocket of his new, brown hunting coat. His fingers felt the cold brass of a .20 gauge shell in the webbing of his pocket. Christopher removed it and examined it idly. It was buckshot for his new shotgun, and it was bound in hard, red paper with shiny gold casing at the primer. To him it was a symbol of his liberation and adventure, and it felt good to roll it in the palm of his hand. He tossed it gently in the air as the headlights bounced upon a pickup truck parked on the side of the road.

"Is that Mr. Fox?" asked Christopher.

"Yes," said Conrad, stopping.

"Do we have to stop, Dad?"

"Yeah, got to visit some. Can't be rude."

Christopher was jealous of his father's time and hated these "visits" with people. They made him uncomfortable. *Damn politics*, he thought.

They got out and walked up to the group of hunters standing in a huddle beside Fox's pickup.

The truck's interior light shone brightly, outlining their faces in an eerie chiaroscuro.

"Morning, Senator," said Fox as they approached.

"Morning, Jim."

"Ready to go?"

"You bet. Any dogs loose yet?" asked Conrad.

"Ain't heard none yet."

"They'll be a'loose soon," said one of the men in Fox's party.

"I thought I heard one a'running in them bottoms, but I ain't so shore now. But they'll be running directly," said Fox with an air of deep seriousness, hands thrust away, deep in his tattered overalls.

"You running any dogs this year, Senator?" asked another.

"Not this year. McPhail always runs enough for everybody."

"Yeah, he shore runs a bunch," said Fox.

"There'll be a heap of em a'running today," added another.

"My oldest boy's got my two dogs. He'll be turning em loose just west of Brushy Creek. They oughta jump something real quick like in there," Fox said.

"Well, we should have a real good race this morning, huh, Jim?" said Conrad.

"Yeah, we'll have that all right," he agreed. "We got a real good crop of deer this year," Fox grinned, revealing several snaggled teeth swimming in tobacco juice.

"Yeah, I've seen a lot around," said Conrad.

"They'll be a whole bunch of them buggers killed today," added Fox, punctuating this observation by spitting a large brown wad into the bushes. This was quickly followed up with a loud clearing of his throat and nose and yet another spitting of tobacco juice and phlegm. After this was completed, he turned to Christopher.

"You ready to get em, boy?"

"Yes, sir," said Christopher, embarrassed. *Mr. Fox always smells of wood smoke in the winter*, thought Christopher, *tobacco and wood smoke*.

"What kind of gun you got, boy?"

"Twenty gauge, got it for my birthday."

"Well, that'll do the trick if you hit him just right. Got to hit him clean enough. Right behind the shoulder."

"Yes, sir," answered Christopher quietly as his gaze fixed upon Fox's surviving front teeth.

"Where y'all going?" asked Fox, turning his attention away from Christopher.

"We'll be just north of this field here in that stand of timber between here and Brushy Creek," answered Conrad.

"You ought to do some good in there. No doubt McPhail's dogs will be drove thew there on both sides of Brushy. We'll be strung just on the other side of it, so amongst us we ought to have a little luck," said Fox, now solemnly adjusting his tobacco lump around to a more comfortable position in the other side of his mouth.

"Y'all might want to cross at the old bridge. The creek's up a little, you know, been real damp this year. We need a little more of that water to fall out of these bottoms."

"Right," agreed Fox, spitting again, this time letting the spittle drool out slowly to the frosty ground and arranging it with his boot. "We'll take the road here and cross up at the bridge while y'all walk the field."

"Good. We'll be just east of that patch of cane bottoms, so y'all'll be clear to shoot to the west," said Conrad, so that there would be no danger of being caught in a cross fire. "No doubt he'll criss-cross the creek trying to shake those dogs if they get him headed thataway to start with," he added.

"Sounds all right. We'll be just north of you on the other side of the creek," nodded Fox. "One of us ought to have a little luck."

"We better get her a'going," said one of the men behind Fox.

"Yup," someone else mumbled.

"Well, you and the boy have a good one," said Fox as if he hadn't heard.

"Thanks. Same to y'all," said Conrad.

"Well, fellas, let's get a move on if we aim to hunt this morning," said Fox while he lifted his rifle out of the truck's gun rack.

"See ya," said Conrad, turning away.

"Right."

"Let's get our gear, Son," said Conrad as he and Christopher walked back to the truck.

The men gathered up their guns, said goodbye, and walked quietly down the road with Fox in the lead.

Conrad was pleased that this was done with a minimum of noise, and he was quick to contrast this with the usual racket and banging about done by other men.

After Fox disappeared, Christopher and his father picked up their guns, adjusted their clothes, and walked into the field. They proceeded about one hundred yards, then turned in the direction of the timber line at the other end.

Conrad was setting a brisk pace in an effort to make it to the far tree line, so Christopher shouldered his shotgun and hurried along as he struggled to keep up. The footing was difficult as Christopher stumbled over the furrows that lay in regular, undulating waves across the field. He wondered if they would make it across and into the foilage before shooting time at first light. Suddenly, Conrad stopped and gazed into the mist hovering above the frozen ground.

"Look," said Conrad in a low whisper, pointing directly ahead with his rifle.

Christopher stared into the greying light that revealed only the plowed brown earth mingling in the morning haze.

"Look just in the edge of the field," said Conrad as he now was looking through the rifle's telescopic sight.

Christopher strained his eyes trying to sweep away the darkness and fog, but he saw nothing.

"You see that big oak tree?"

"Where?"

"Just visible in the tree line."

"Yes, I see it now."

"Well, look just two fingers to the right of that," said Conrad holding two fingers and sighting down them, squinting with one eye closed.

Christopher did likewise, and now he saw a small black object that he had not seen before.

"I think I see it, I see it," said Christopher in an excited whisper.

"Here, look through this," said Conrad as he handed him the rifle. Dropping to one knee, Christopher lifted the rifle to his shoulder and looked into the scope. Through the increasing light, he could see the cross-hairs move around a young whitetail buck. Christopher's heavy breathing and rapid heartbeat bounced the sight about dizzily, and he could not count the number of points on the antlers.

"It's a buck, right."

"You bet."

"He's out of range, huh, Dad?"

"Just a little."

"How did you ever see him?"

"We need to go," said Conrad, noticing that it was practically daylight.

Christopher stood up and they resumed their walk toward the trees. After a few steps, he felt a cold breeze on the back of his neck, and within a few seconds, the deer, now clearly visible, raised his head and looked in their direction. Held frozen for a moment, white ears spread gracefully behind his antlers, the buck seemed curious. Then in one fluid, bounding movement, he vanished into the timber behind.

"That was a nice one, huh, Dad?" said Christopher in a loud voice that startled him somewhat after all of the whispering.

"Yes," agreed Conrad, quickening his step.

"Dad, he was beautiful," gasped Christopher as he stumbled along behind, barely keeping pace.

Before Conrad could answer, the sharp report of a rifle abruptly split the air.

"Where was that?"

"Over to the right by the road."

"Do you think that was Mr. Fox, Dad?"

"Let's hurry, Son," answered Conrad, half hearing.

4

CHRISTOPHER AND HIS father stood silently in the forest. It was a woods of hardwood timber and an occasional pine or cedar. Years had passed since it had been "cutover" and, while there were thickets of underbrush, briars, and saplings, the forest had large "den trees" and hardwood oaks and hickory that stood in quiet, almost timeless dignity at the gates of Bayou Blanc Bottoms.

Conrad had carefully selected this position before the season. It was located in a small clearing under a large oak tree about fifty yards into the woods, and Brushy Creek could be seen through the trees and thicket to the north of them. Conrad knew that the dogs would likely be driven from the west, and any deer would have to pass by the line of hunters on either side of the creek. He felt it was unlikely that one could get by them unseen.

"How'd you pick this spot, Dad?" asked Christopher, as he leaned against a small tree cradling his gun in his arms, his breath smoking in the air.

"Well, Son, a deer will try to avoid that field, go around it to the north, which means he'll more than likely come through this stand of timber we're in here. He might be on one side of the creek or the other. If he comes south of it, then we'll have a chance to get a shot."

"I see."

"The wind is out of the south, which is why that buck smelled us earlier, and a buck is afraid of his down-wind side, so he'll try to keep a little brush between himself and wherever it is he can't smell. He can smell into the field but not into the brush, so he'll skirt the north edge of this field with a good thicket down wind for protection. It's their nature."

"Will a doe do the same thing?"

"Much more careless."

"Why?"

"Not hunted so much, and I think they just get tamer and less cautious."

"They aren't ever legal, huh, Dad?"

31

"Nope, just now and then when they overpopulate," Conrad said as he set his rifle against the big white oak tree and placed his hands into his jeans pockets.

"Reckon we'll get a shot?"

"Might."

"He'll come in a flash, huh?"

"If the dogs are close, he'll be stepping out."

"Not much time for a shot?"

"No, but don't get nervous. Just hold em and squeeze em."

"You going to let me shoot, Dad?"

"Sure. I'm not even going to pick up my rifle unless he's out of range for you."

"You going to tell me to shoot or not?"

"I'll say if it's a buck or doe. After that, it's up to you to take your own shot as you see it. Take a good shot, won't get much more than one."

"Can I have it mounted?"

"Let's get one first," laughed Conrad.

"I'd like to have it mounted." ·

"If it's a big buck, we'll have it mounted."

"How big?"

"At least three points on each side."

"You figure Mom'll let me put it in my room?"

"We'll work on her."

It was completely light now, and occasional shots began to crack through the morning air. One pack of dogs could be heard in the distance.

"I hear some dogs," said Christopher.

"Sounds like they might be McPhail's. That's just about where he'd turn em loose."

"Are they coming this way?"

"I think so."

They stood silently for a while, listening to the race as the sound of the baying drew closer.

Christopher could think of nothing more fun than being here in the woods with his father. Not having any brothers or sisters, he felt close to him, and to Barrel; they were his older brothers, his after-school companions, as well as his tutors.

Now that he was twelve and had his own gun, this truly was his first fall. It was an initiation.

The dogs grew louder. Christopher looked admiringly at his father standing tall under the great oak. He had a curious habit of placing his tongue under his lower lip, like a lump of tobacco, when he meant business in a happy way, and now the lip stuck out.

"Beautiful, ain't it?" said Christopher, realizing how much Conrad was enjoying it.

"It's a hot one sure'nuf, but it sounds like they're on the other side of the creek, the north side."

"Reckon it's a buck?"

"Don't know. Could be," said Conrad, moving slowly toward his rifle.

As they stood silently, a brown thrush lit in an elm sapling and looked at them, curiously cocking his head from one side to the other. Conrad picked up his rifle and cradled it in the crook of his arm as the baying of the dogs grew closer.

"What do you think, Dad?"

"Can't tell. Let's be real quiet and still," he said in a whisper.

An unexpected succession of rapid shots rang out on the other side of the creek.

"Fox, huh? They killed it."

"No, I think they missed."

"Why?"

"Too many shots and the dogs are still coming."

"Where. . ."

"Shhh," admonished Conrad, holding his fingers to his lips.

The sound of the dogs suddenly changed directions, and veered toward them.

"They are coming this way. Shots turned him," Conrad said in a hush.

Barrel was right. "One shot a deer, two shots maybe, and three a miss," thought Christopher.

"I think we may get a crack at him, Son."

They heard more splashes from the direction of the creek.

"Is that him crossing the creek?" whispered Christopher.

"No, it's the dogs. He's already across, coming this way."

Christopher shifted, anxiously fingering the red safety button behind the trigger guard.

"Be ready," Conrad warned in a quiet, steady voice.

They heard more shots, too far away to be at their animal but moving quickly towards them. The barking of the dogs grew louder as they crossed the creek and renewed the chase.

"Any time now," whispered Conrad.

Christopher felt his heart moving against his wool shirt and his hands sweating in his gloves as he strained to listen. He slipped the safety off with a loud click; it seemed deafening in the quiet tension under the oak tree.

The brown thrush flew away.

Suddently Conrad caught a glimpse of a small shadow moving in the trees and brush. Like a phantom, it moved quietly, disappearing, and reappearing, back and forth, like a half-remembered dream.

"Over there," he said, barely audible.

"Where?"

"There, he'll pass to our right," he said, pointing to where the shadow had been.

A twig broke, and the tiny specter transformed itself into an animal running effortlessly through the thicket near the creek.

"Look, look, look," Conrad said, spitting the words out rapidly. The deer leaped into the clearing, stopped, and stared at them with brave eyes. It was a very young buck with small, spike horns.

"Shoot, shoot," ordered Conrad.

Christopher could not move. He simply stared. The dogs closed the distance, the deer snorted, then bounded out of the clearing into the nearby undergrowth.

"Shoot! Son! Shoot!"

Christopher awoke from his trance, found his arms, and hastily fired an unaimed shot. Excited, he didn't feel the recoil of the automatic, but aimed and fired again and again at the tail that flashed like a man waving a white handkerchief in the trees.

"Well, I'll be damn," he heard Conrad say behind him.

Christopher lowered his gun. He felt weak and now wished immediately for a second chance.

"Missed."

"Yes," replied Christopher in a meek voice.

"You certainly gave him a real good send off. Sure did."

"Dad, I don't know what happened. Just got kind of excited, I guess."

"Little nervous, huh?"

"Yes, like I was paralyzed."

"Weak all over?"

"And numb."

"Stomach churning and heart pounding?"

"That's it exactly."

"Sweating a real cold, clammy kind of sweat, too, huh?"

"How did you know?"

"You got it all right. No doubt about it."

"Got what?" asked Christopher turning a little pale.

"Buck fever."

"What?"

"Buck fever. As bad a case I've ever seen. You got all the classic symptoms. Pounding heart, weak kneed, you got em all, sure do."

"Buck fever, huh?"

"Yup, and you sure got it and got it bad."

"What is buck fever, Dad?"

"Well, it's a strange and terrible kind of malady that afflicts a body when he sees that easy shot at a deer, usually for the first time. It infects the nervous system and paralyzes a man. Just like you a minute ago."

"How do you catch it?"

"Lying awake at night and dreaming about deer hunting, that's how. If you do that, you'll catch it every time without a doubt."

"What's the cure?"

"May not be any. Sometimes it's incurable; some folks just have to give up hunting on account of it."

"Come on, Dad, shoot straight."

"I am shooting straight. Yours may just be a hopeless case, may never get well."

"All I need is a second chance."

"May just happen again. Like I say, some folks never get over it."

"Come on."

"There is one cure that works now and then though."

"What's that?"

"Well. . ."

"I know. Cut the shirttail off, huh? I've heard Barrel talk about that for people who miss an easy shot. Kinda like this 'buck fever' you say I've got so bad. That's it, isn't it?"

"No, some folks believe in that shirttail business, but I think it only makes it worse."

"What is it then?"

"Well, you got to go hunting again that very same day. Better in the evening with your dad, if he's available, and let him show you how it's done. And if you're successful, it will cure you every time, never seen it to fail."

"Can we go this evening, no kidding."

"You bet."

"Got a place picked out?"

"Sure do. I figured we might need a buck fever cure, so I got a field in mind where Barrel says they've been feeding."

"What the heck, this was only a little ole spike anyway, huh?"

"Yeah, we'll find us a big deer this evening. Save that little ole spike for next year, when he'll be a real deer."

"We'll just say, if anybody asks, that he was a little bit out of range, a real tough shot and running like the dickens."

"Just a real hard shot on a small one. Don't want anybody hearing that buck fever is going around. People'll treat you different like if they think you're a carrier or something."

As Christopher reloaded his gun, four black-and-tan hounds trotted into the clearing, baying in confusion. They sniffed about in the leaves where the deer had been, then one, finding the scent, let out a low bawling moan and disappeared into the thicket with the others quickly behind.

Christopher and his father remained long enough for a pair of doe to trot aimlessly by; then gave up and went home.

5

THEY HEARD LATER that Fox had missed.

Lunch was always something of a banquet at the Shaw table. Today there was a large smoked ham sitting partly sliced in the center, surrounded by plates of fried chicken, potato salad, cole slaw, tomatoes, cucumbers, greens, onions, cornbread, white bread, rye bread, gravy, fried squirrel, butter, and cherry pie. Everybody drank iced tea even though it was December; of course, there was coffee for everybody who might want it; kept as it always was in a pot by the stove. What was not eaten that day would be put up and served later. All the meat and vegetables came from the farm except the squirrel that Barrel Bradford kept on everybody's plate during the cool months. Queeny would "deep fry" it like chicken rolling it in flour mixed with butter and eggs. Sometimes when Barrel was in a hurry for lunch he would put several pieces of squirrel into half a milk carton and eat out of it like a popcorn box. Usually, he would remember to spit out his tobacco first and rinse his mouth. He said that tobacco ruined the taste of any meat, and Queeny "worked too hard to ruin her squirrel with a chaw of nasty ole tobacco."

"We gonna cure your buck fever this evening, Son, that's for certain," said Conrad slicing the ham and putting it on Christopher's plate.

"Well, Fox won't be heard bragging, huh, Dad?"

"Nope, but he'll have his before the season's over. He does every year."

"Doesn't he work any, Dad?"

"Not this week he won't, he always takes off the whole week."

"He'll be in the woods every day, huh?"

"Before an after dark."

"Barrel told Queeny and me that he has a place scouted out for you all," said Elizabeth pouring Conrad's coffee.

"Yup, he does, got em spotted in an ole field near that bottom land timber."

"We gonna use dogs?"

"No, not this evening. We'll crawl Indian-like down wind of em. This'll be different kind of huntin from what you've seen, in some ways it's more fun. There's really more to it than using dogs."

"That's the way my daddy liked to hunt all the time," Elizabeth added sitting down. "The only thing he ever ran with dogs was a coon or a fox."

"It takes more skill than dogs, really does," said Conrad, taking a large bite of sandwich.

"Mister Conrad, you be lucky if'n Barrel hit a lick this morning with all that scouting he be doing, I bet he ain't done nothing. You know how he is when the firs fros stick an them ole dogs get to moanin and mouthin in them bottoms, why, he can't stand it," said Queeny from behind the stove where she was busy cleaning.

"That's all right, I can't fault em there. Got to have meat on the table don't we Queeny, got to eat."

"Yas, suh, Barrel'll an y'all have us cookin wild meat till we done forgotten what a cow taste like, sho will."

"I've got to go into Frenchman's Bluff to see Wilbur Webb bout business, but I'll be back in time to hunt this evening. You an Barrel load some of that hay from the small barn till I get back, okay?"

"Yes, sir," replied Christopher solemnly.

"Mister Conrad, you be lucky to get Barrel's mind on any kind 'a hay loading today, not with what he got his mind on," said Queeny.

"Chores can't wait forever, we've got to get something done Queeny."

"Yes, suh, I knows that, but Barrel ain't no count these days; I been married to em too long to be any kind fool bout that."

"How bout let's do it tomorrow, Dad?"

"Nope, today. You'll get through in time, I'll see to that. I'll come get you."

"Well don't get all tied up with Mr. Webb an forget."

"Don't worry, we'll have deer meat hanging on the hoof by in the morning."

After lunch Christopher and Barrel drove the pickup truck down toward the hay barn.

The pickup was a battered veteran, blue with rust trimming. It carried a fuel tank with a pump and nozzle that sat "flush" with the cab. Its bed supported an oily mixture of manure, rotten hay and mud that seemed to just grow there despite occasional attempts to clean it up. The interior housed a ripped seat, broken radio, busted speedometer, and a doorless glove compartment. On the dashboard was an assortment of oily rags, pliers, work gloves, two shotgun shells, a screwdriver, rusty flashlight battery, an empty Lone Star beer can that rattled next to the window, and a pencil that was stuck in the defrost vent.

"How do you want to work it?" yelled Christopher as they approached the dilapidated two-storied barn.

"Well, let's see. One of us has gots to drop the hay out of the lof and the other one gots to load it in the truck. Ain't that right?" yelled Barrel back, as they tried to speak over the engine whose muffler had been "stumped" herding cows.

"Right."

"What you like to do?"

"You're the hay-loader," hollered Christopher, his ears ringing.

"All right, since you the lest one, why don't you climb up into the lof, and I'll be down in the truck to do the stacking."

"Fine with me, Barrel,"said Christopher pretending not to care.

"Good. Let me back this truck up against the side of the barn afore you gets up in the lof," said Barrel as he double-clutched and ground the gears into reverse, backing it underneath the loft door.

Christopher got out and climbed into the hay loft as Barrel waited patiently below. After a time, Christopher emerged at the portal with a bale of hay held firmly by the binding rope.

"Okay, throw it down," yelled Barrel, now standing in the truck bed, his backside resting against the fuel tank.

With both hands on the rope, Christopher lifted it and, kicking it with his knee, pushed the bale in one awkward lurch to Barrel's direction who stepped back as the hay bounced into the truck.

"That's good; keep bringing em on," said Barrel, adjusting the bale slightly.

Barrel sat on the solitary bale and waited for the maneuver to be repeated. After a time, Christopher reappeared, and the hay plopped clumsily into the truck.

"How many we got now?" asked Christopher, the fifth bale held firmly in hand as he panted in the cool air.

"I counts five," replied Barrel, sitting comfortably, arms folded.

Christopher threw it into the truck bed, and Barrel arranged it without having to lift anything.

"How long we been working?" asked Barrel, wiping off his forehead with a dirty sleeve. "I reckon we been working bout twenty minutes."

"That all? Damn, seems like forever," said Christopher.

"Look here, Mr. Chris, I'm a little tired after all this work, so come on down, and let's take a res," said Barrel, jumping out of the truck to the ground.

"Good idea," added Christopher, climbing down the ladder and walking over to the truck.

"Barrel, I believe you found yourself a good job down here in this truck, stacking these bales of hay for me, huh?"

"What you mean by that, Mr. Chris?"

"You know what I mean," grinned Christopher, eying the bales stacked in the bed.

"Now, Mr. Chris, standing in that ole lof is easy. All you gots to do is throw em down to me, an I does all the liftin an totin. It's this heavy stacking that gets you," said Barrel, rubbing his lower back.

Christopher emptied the hay out of his hat and scratched under his collar.

"Listen, Barrel, let's me and you trade off. What do you say? I'm ready to do some of the hard work — you know liftin and totin."

"Yes, suh, we can trade off, in jes uh minute, but to be fair like, let's do that jes as soon as we gets a few mo of them ole bales loaded into the truck."

"Right, then there'll really be some stacking to do," he said, looking hard at

Barrel.

"Now, now, Mr. Chris, all I'm trying to do is teach you bout hay-loadin which you don't seem to understand or know nothin about and got to know if'n you gonna to be any count. You want to amount to sumpin when you is grown, don't you?"

"Mr. Barrel, I can't tell you how much I appreciate it, because next time I know who's getting the easy job in the damn loft first, and who's gonna be unlucky enough to do the liftin an totin down in the truck."

"Don't start no cussing now, cause Miss Elizabeth be blaming me if'n she hear you. She say you get's all that ole stuff from the 'hands,' which mean me, and I don't want to hear you doing no kind of cussin," said Barrel, with mock alarm.

"You sure doing a whole lot of teaching for one day, huh? Teaching me about hay-loading and cussin, all at once like. You reckon I can learn all this in one day, huh, Barrel?"

"Why, sho I do. I'm thirty-six year old. I can splain lots of things to you, if'n you listen an ain't too uppity an hard-headed an actin like all ole Barrel wants to do is fool you," laughed Barrel as he leaned against the cab of the truck and put his rough hands into his overall pockets.

"Why don't you teach me something worthwhile? Hay-loadin ain't no fun, and I ain't going to ever quit cussin, hard as I try. I know that cause I already tried a hun'erd times."

"*Everything* can't be fun, Mr. Chris. You gots to learn something that folks needs for you to make a livin, and that ain't *ever* fun. If it was, you couldn't make a livin at it. You gots to *make* yo fun when you gets time, when you can finds it, that's the way life is, and there ain't no heppin it."

"We're going to hunt this evening, though, huh, Barrel?"

"What you talking bout, boy? We going to tear em up, that's fo sho."

"You got a buck staked out?"

"I gots a big buck picked out jes for us and Mr. Conrad. I knows right where he's at, and ain't nobody been round there neither."

"Reckon they might of gotten him today, Barrel?"

"Listen, I'm the only ones that knows where he at, when he comes and when he goes, jes me. I done had him picked out for a long time, and I been tippin round watchin em. But we gots to be quiet, and we needs to crawl up on him jes fo it get dark. Jes like a bunch of Indians in the movies. Gots to do it jes right."

"How big is he?"

"Ooooweee, he looks like one of them big elks you gots pictures of hangin on yo wall; that's how big he is. Like you see on the front of them magazines you is always reading."

"Where does he stay?"

"Deep in them ole bottoms, that's where. That's where all the big bucks stays. Then he comes to the fields early in the morning and late in the evening, and he's real smart and skittish. Deer an folks jes alike; they gets into little habits without really knowin nothing bout it. You sticks with ole Barrel; tween me and Mr. Conrad, we'll teach you sumpin bout hunting, sho will."

"Dad says now that I got my gun I can hunt all the time."

"You gettin to the age to get serious bout it all right. Time to quit foolin around. We teach you all you needs to know, yes suh, we can do that. I can teach you sumpin else too," he said with a chuckle.

"What's that?" asked Christopher, cocking his head at Barrel with friendly suspicion. "You got something in mind, Barrel, I can see the laughing in your eyes."

"I can teach you how to kill a mess of rabbits faster 'n you can say it."

"How we gonna hunt rabbits and we ain't got nothing with us but buck-shot?"

"Mr. Chris, you think that ole Barrel been hunting all his long life an come here to the field with nothing but buckshot? Is that what you think? Boy, I gots more to teach you than I done owned up to. We gots work to do with you boy."

"Now, Barrel, how we going to do hay-loading if we go rabbit hunting? Tell me that. Huh?"

Barrel reached into the cab of the truck and handed Christopher his shotgun.

"We ain't," laughed Barrel. "It's fun time now."

6

CONRAD WAS WAITING at the wire gap by the hog lot when they drove up. Barrel stopped the truck next to Conrad who was leaning against a fence post.

"Afternoon, Mr. Conrad," said Barrel, turning off the engine and rolling down the window as far as it would go, which was only halfway.

"Afternoon. Y'all finished?" said Conrad eyeing the six bales in the back of the truck.

"Not quite. We got a little mo to do jes yet."

Conrad glanced at Christopher. "How about you, were you any help?"

"Yes, sir, Barrel showed me how to help him."

"Yes, suh, he was a powerful help, sho was, a real help."

"I notice you didn't forget your guns," said Conrad, looking at the two shotguns slung in the window rack. "See anything?"

"Well, we thought we might hunt a little if'n we got finished real quick like. Can't ever tell, it being deer season."

"I reckon this is your third or fourth trip, huh?"

"No, suh, this here's our first trip."

"First trip?" said Conrad.

"Yes, suh, our first trip," said Barrel, fingering the gear shift with a gloved thumb.

Conrad eyed Christopher who was quiet, while Barrel took off his hat and pretended to dust it.

"Y'all must of left plenty of hay in that barn then?"

"Oh, yes, suh, there's plenty of hay in that barn. We gots lots of hay," said Barrel with enthusiasm. "All the hay we needs. Them cows'll have plenty to eat this winter fo sho."

Conrad looked back in the bed of the truck and spotted a brown towsack lying in the corner next to a bale of hay. He picked it up and looked inside. There was silence in the cab.

"You say there's lots of hay left in that barn?" he asked.

"Yes, suh, plenty of hay," replied Barrel. "Sho is."

"Not many rabbits left round there though, huh?"

"No, suh, we was hell on them rabbits," smiled Barrel meekly. "Sho was. We burned em up."

"I guess Christopher must have run you crazy about going rabbit hunting, till you just broke down and took him, right."

"Yes, suh, Mr. Chris just bout ran me slap out of my mind bout taking him to hunt them durned ole rabbits. I didn't want to go but I jes threw up my hands an said, 'Okay, you gonna get me into a heap of trouble,' sho did, 'but gets your gun and let's go,' and that's the way it happened. Yes, suh, sho is, just like that," said Barrel.

"Is that right, Christopher?" asked Conrad.

"Yes,sir, after Barrel taught me all about hay-loadin, liftin-n-totin, well, I just got all over his nerves about taking me rabbit hunting cause there ain't anybody who knows more about hunting rabbits than Barrel here," said Christopher. "Sure enough, that's the way it happened, Dad. I just got on to poor Barrel and wouldn't let him go, just about run him raggedy."

"That's right, Mr. Conrad, this boy just bout run me rickety," added Barrel. "I was jes helpless. Sho was."

"Paralyzed, huh?" said Conrad.

"Oh, Mr. Conrad, I was worse than that; I couldn't even move."

"Snakebit, right?"

"Oooh, yes, suh, that boy of yo's is like a big ole cotton mouf when it comes to poisoning a body away from work," said Barrel.

"Yeah, and Mr. Barrel here is like death on them rabbits," laughed Christopher. "Six shells, an six rabbits. Big ole swamp rabbits too, I ain't ever seen rabbits that big. So big they jes bout had me scared!"

"Yes, suh, them is *eatin* rabbits, couldn't hardly shoot for my mouf a waterin," said Barrel.

Conrad tossed the towsack back into the bed of the truck.

"Well, that hay'll keep till after hunting season, won't it, Barrel?"

"Yes, suh, and if'n we kills one this evenin, I won't even need to wait till then. But we can't just let this season slip by, lessen we gets us a big buck, not with as many as we been seeing all year an can't do nothing but look at em," said Barrel.

"Well, just as soon as y'all give those rabbits to Queeny for cleaning, the sooner we can get going. It'll be getting dark soon."

"Won't take but a minute, Mr. Conrad. Queeny'll fix em so we'll have sumpin to eat with all them venisons we gonna have after this evening," said Barrel quickly starting the engine.

"I'll have Miss Elizabeth fix us sandwiches so we won't miss supper," said Conrad. "Let's hurry now."

"I'll get the light and skinning knife and be right back to the house," said Barrel.

"Christopher, you come with me. You need to visit with your mother before we leave again; you can tell her about the rabbit hunt with Barrel," said Conrad, trying to speak over the engine. Christopher got out, and Barrel quickly drove away through the shallow black mud and hog manure.

7

THE LIGHT WAS SUBMITTING gently to darkness as Christopher crept through the forest behind his father and Barrel. Armed only with a small skinning knife, Barrel led them slowly along a faint, almost invisible trail. They were in a large stand of timber near a meadow, approaching it down wind. Conrad shifted his rifle to the crook of his arm and leaned over Barrel's shoulder. Christopher kept a few steps in back. Barrel had stopped and was kneeling in the shadow of a poplar tree that waved in the cold evening air. With two black fingers, he pressed aside a blade of grass that had concealed a single deer track and smiled a broad smile.

"Look," he whispered proudly.

"Fresh," answered Conrad, now on one knee beside him.

"Real fresh. Big, too," Barrel said as the shadow of leaves danced across his face.

"Might be our buck."

"Yes, suh, too big to be a doe. This the way he usually come in. It's him. Can't be any other."

Conrad turned and motioned for Christopher.

"Look, Son, here," said Conrad in a hush. Christopher stooped over his father's shoulder as he pointed to the track.

"Dad, that's beautiful," said Christopher in a whisper.

Conrad, leaning on his rifle for support, reached forward and brushed aside another clump of grass that was hanging over the path revealing another, smaller print.

"Is that a doe?" asked Christopher.

"Either that or a spike," said Conrad.

"Probably one or two does moving in front of this here ole buck," said Barrel, looking along the trail.

"We better move along before it gets too dark," said Conrad.

"Yes, suh, we gots to get there real quick. Don't want folks thinkin we shootin no deer after it get dark," said Barrel getting up and moving quietly down the spoor.

Near the clearing, Barrel signaled for them to drop to the ground. He lay prone behind a thin sapling while the others crawled up on their hands and knees.

"There," he whispered, pointing into the meadow shrouded now by the fading light and shadow.

Conrad stared through the trees into the clearing. The woods were dark, but the meadow was dimly lit, as if by a yellow flood light.

"Yes, there're three," he said, pointing in the direction of a trio of gray, slender forms on the edge of the field just beyond the hardwood trees.

"Yes, suh, three," agreed Barrel. "It's gettin awfully dark quick. Got's to move on up next to em. Light's going fast."

"Yeah, we need to move a little closer."

"Too far for a shot?" asked Christopher.

"Yeah, not enough light for this sight. We'll have to get closer. Hope the wind doesn't change," said Conrad.

Christopher started when a screech owl shattered the eerie calm from a perch deep in the woods. Lying face down, he breathed heavily into the dead weeds, not moving. He could smell wet ground and the rotting fall grass. The air was cold, but he was sweating. A woodpecker banged on a hollow tree.

"Christopher, Christopher," whispered his father still lying prone but slightly ahead.

"Sir?" he answered, raising his head slowly, hurting the muscles in his neck.

"Come on, Son. We need to crawl closer. Stay near me, okay?"

"Yes, sir," said Christopher, looking at the gray form of his father's rump rising like a small mountain above the dirty soles of his hunting boots.

The sun was disappearing quickly in the west, as Conrad, rifle cradled in arms, crawled ahead, leading them on their stomachs under an old barbed wire fence that stood watch round the meadow. Christopher felt the rusty barbs scrape the back of his coat as he inched under the limply hanging wire, straining his neck upward to see over the grass now dead from the December frost. About a hundred yards away, Christopher saw the buck raise its head. Conrad and Barrel froze. Christopher was caught stretching his neck awkwardly with the barbed wire still scratching against his back. The deer gave one ear a nervous twitch and glanced to the left then quickly turned his head alertly back towards them. Absolutely still, he stood ignoring his left, caressed as it was by a breeze, but fearful of the timber where a strange noise had beat itself against the wind. A pair of doe continued to browse as the sun sank behind the trees, abandoning the scene to near darkness. Christopher hoped that the buck would not notice his breath smoking in the cold air and wished, too, that all he could see were some rather odd-shaped lumps sitting incongruously on the edge of the field.

The owl screamed again as if announcing a change of scene in some primeval ritual – acknowledged now by the buck stomping a nervous foot on the hard ground. The woodpecker hushed. The owl screeched again, then again, sending a shudder through Christopher as it seemed closer than before, more mysterious and solitary in the dark forest. It was blacker; the flood light was going out.

"What if I were alone? I couldn't stand it," Christopher thought, watching the buck lower his head to the ground and begin to graze once more.

Christopher saw the front clump unravel into the shape of a sitting man, elbows resting on knees, under a long stick-like object that protruded forward. He felt the grass under his heart move again, while he held his breath. then an explosion shattered the air, and flame burst from Conrad's rifle, almost unnaturally, like no thunder or sound he had ever heard before. The noise cracked through the field like the unexpected rumble of an unseen storm, clearing everything before it as one shadow dropped and two bounded quickly away.

"Ooooweee, you done hit him a lick," Barrel hollered loudly almost dancing as he ran ahead. Christopher freed himself from the wire tearing his coat, then jumped to his feet in time to see the doe clear the fence and disappear into the wood's dark embrace.

"Is he dead?" asked Conrad as he and Christopher hurried up to Barrel, standing by the deer.

"Sho nuf is. You caught him just right. He sho is pretty; I counts four points on each side," said Barrel as he knelt down beside the buck and caressed his antlers gently. "We sho was lucky; few mo minutes and it would be past shootin time."

"It's pretty close. I couldn't use my sight, just aimed down the side of the barrel."

"That was a mighty good shot, Mr. Conrad. I reckon it was more than a hundred yards; that was a powerful good shot," bragged Barrel, still inspecting the antlers.

"Great shot, Dad. It sure was loud enough," blurted Christopher, his ears ringing.

"That's cause it so quiet, and you so excited," grinned Barrel. "I know'd they be back this evening. They ain't hardly been no hunting round here, and they jes loves this patch of clearing. We gonna have enough venisons for all the rest of the year."

"I thought the only thing that you were interested in was rabbit meat," said Conrad, laughing.

"Shit, I'm gonna throw that durned ole rabbit meat to the dowgs after today. We gonna have bar-be-que venisons, stewed venisons, fried venisons, and every other kind of venison meat there is. Yes, suh, we gonna work Queeny slap to death, cookin and fryin venisons. Sho is."

Christopher switched on the flashlight and swept the beam of light up and down the body of the buck.

The antlers were perfectly formed into a rack of eight points; four on each side. His head was lying with a slight rightward twist, the mouth open, allowing the tongue to lick the grass with a speck of bright blood. The light brown hide was smooth with white under-trim, interrupted only by a small hole behind the shoulder that expanded into a much larger one on the opposite side. He smelled and felt warm in the grass as Christopher knelt

45

down and examined him with his light. *Blood has a peculiar smell*, he thought.

"He sure is pretty," said Christopher, touching the horn delicately.

"Mr. Conrad, we gonna have a good year. Why, we nearly got the crops laid by, and we gots plenty of deer, and rabbit and squirrel. We might even get aloose some night and run us a big ole boar coon, yes, suh. And Mr. Chris here is getting big enough to carry hisself. We gonna have a good year; I knows it," said Barrel. "Yes, suh, sho is."

"Yeah, Barrel, we sure are. And we're starting this deer season off right; you sure did a good job scouting," said Conrad. "Real good job."

"I just kinda fooled round in here when I could shake aloose some, but we was lucky today."

"Yeah, sure were," said Conrad as he unloaded his rifle, ejecting the brass casing.

"Yes, suh, things sure gonna end up good this year; I just knows it," said Barrel. "Ain't gonna be snake bit like we was las year."

After a few minutes, Conrad and Barrel cut a sapling, tied the buck to it, and started home with Christopher in the lead, shining his light ahead in the starless night.

8

CORPORAL NGUYEN VAN TIEN wished very much that he were home too as he crimped the barbed wire with the pliers, then slowly worked it with his fingers until it quietly snapped. The Marines had tied empty Coca-Cola cans filled with pebbles in the wire and now one of them rattled to his right. The rain had stopped and there was no wind, so Nguyen was frightened by the noise. He held his breath hoping the Marines had not heard. Suddenly a flare rocketed out over the wire making him flinch. Nguyen closed his eyes tightly and dropped his head to the earth, freezing his body like a shadow. The enemy had burned around the wire to destroy the tall grass and Nguyen told his men to roll in the soot for camouflage. He hoped that the muddy ash on their bodies would save them. More flares shot out, filling the night sky with light. "Damn," he said, his lips moving in the mud.

Uncle Nhang had fought the French at Dien Bien Phu and he said "flares were good because they destroyed the enemy's night vision; once they started they would have to keep it up until dawn." Nguyen wondered. He wished the flares had not started at all and he closed his eyelids even tighter and hugged the earth smelling the burned grass. Mortar flares popped out as well as the little illumination rockets shot by the infantry; it was like the sun had come early. Nguyen was in the edge of the wire with the squad hidden in a small ditch fifty yards behind; their mission was to move in close and set up a base of fire for the sappers to assault into Fox Company's compound with their satchel charges. Nguyen was convinced that the Coke can had ruined the attack. More flares. Suddenly M-16s started shooting and screams came from the right where a few minutes before the can had faintly rattled its pebbles. An AK-47 answered back but was quickly smothered by machine gun fire from a bunker. Tracers zipped over Nguyen's head. The attack was ruined. Mortar fire came from both sides, and satchel charges started exploding deeper in the concertina wire; the air was filled with more screams and automatic rifle fire. *They're going in anyway, the fools*, thought Nguyen. *Sappers are crazy.* The weapons continued at a rapid pitch; Nguyen tried to melt into the earth. He thought, *No use trying to bring the squad up, they'll be slaughtered. Got to be patient and wait for time to get back. Must move the squad back before the helicopters and jets come. They will come with the sun, they always do. But I must be patient.*

There was moaning in the wire where the can had rattled. Some words yelled out in a strange language and even stranger laughter. More M-16 fire. The moaning stopped. The sappers had tried to go too fast. *Crazy sappers.*

The flares continued steadily but fewer in number, so Nguyen waited for the nearest to burn out; then he began to inch backwards, crawling toward the ditch, stopping with each flare that came nearby. They floated in silhouette across the earth and when each burned out striking the ground behind, their parachutes folding up gracefully, he would move, then freeze again. More flares, more light, then more brief periods of darkness and slowly Nguyen made his way back to his squad.

The hill on the left was quiet. There was an occasional flare but no firing. The Lieutenant had said that the enemy had its Battalion Headquarters there, and it was very well defended. Orders were to attack Fox Company instead; it was known as a "hard luck" outfit and might be easier to engage. *They did not act like a 'hard luck' unit at all, not today,* Nguyen thought. *We are the ones with the 'hard luck' this morning with those crazy sappers and that damn Coke can jiggling the alarm. The Marines were awake; we had hoped to catch them asleep. Activity has deliberately decreased for weeks so that the Americans would get careless; but it hasn't worked, at least not here with Fox Company.*

Now an engine started, a big one, a tank. *Where? Oh, yes, on the left, the hill over there, but it cannot move.* Tanks. Nguyen hated them. The engine idled for a minute and then it moved to another position and stopped. *Changing around. Very clever. We spot them during the day and they move them around at night,* he thought. *I'm glad Fox does not have tanks. They won't shoot them from over there; they are too afraid of killing their own men. Curious. Very strange way to fight.* "Get close to them, hug them close, they don't like to fire on themselves," Uncle Nhang had said. Uncle Nhang had been a good soldier.

Fox Company did not have tanks but they had a 106 recoiless rifle somewhere; he had seen it with the binoculars the day before. It was mounted in a bunker and the sappers had targeted it, but they would never get to it now. *The Marines have not fired the 106, no doubt waiting on a hard target, not wanting to compromise its position. That's smart. These Marines can be good when they aren't busy being complacent. Much better than the Saigon soldiers, much, much better, who are all stupid and cowardly.* Nguyen had heard of some good Saigon outfits, but he had never encountered any. The Lieutenant said the Saigon soldiers could be good if properly led, but Nguyen did not believe it. All the ones he had seen were terrible, and he did not understand why the Americans had so much patience with them.

The squad's ditch was very small. Nguyen had just enough room to squirm in front of the first man. *How long can we wait here?* he wondered. *It'll be dawn soon. The only ones able to fight now are on the hillside where they can hide in tunnels and holes, but we are stuck here in this stupid ditch. There is a Marine Listening Post over there somewhere, and we must be very careful or they will use that 106 on us that they have been so coy with.* Artillery was landing with a *carump, carump, carump,* on the slope behind them.

Damn crazy sappers. Damn crazy war. More artillery landed. Close. Shrapnel splinters cut the air like bird's wings. *The artillery is bad but the bombs are worse. We must move from here and quickly. The signal to withdraw will be the B-40s; when they are shot at Fox Company we must withdraw no matter what,* he concluded. *At least the moon is hidden by the clouds.*

Tomorrow will be a busy day. This offensive must be everywhere so the Americans will have plenty to do tomorrow besides worry with us. The Lieutenant said that we are to go back into the valley tomorrow and hit the villages guarded by the Saigon soldiers; those of us that are left. Yes, tomorrow will be difficult. This offensive must be very big.

The fighting seemed to quieten down for a while. Nguyen passed the word down the line to be ready to go the instant the B-40s started firing. The new man wiggled behind him. "Be still!" he commanded in a forceful whisper. *Replacement,* he thought, *no real training. I've got to help him or he'll never make it.*

It was cold in the little ditch with an inch of water in the bottom. For the first time that night he realized that he was cold. Shivers. He hoped that it was just dampness and not malaria. So many of his comrades had died of malaria since coming into the South, down the trail; it was worse than the bombing in some ways, much worse; at least the bombing was quick and was over–it either got you or it didn't. He was a long way from home. It had made sense fighting the bombers at home near his village, not far from Hanoi, but here, Nguyen did not like it here. *Why die for these damned stupid, ungrateful Southerners?* Besides, his wife had a small child and the village needed him to help with the rice harvest, but instead he was here, somewhere in the South after a long dangerous journey, and now the Americans were intent on killing him if they could. NVA mortars fired back quickly and then silenced themselves. *Good,* he thought, *at least someone is still alive back there.* The water seemed much colder thinking about home. Hadn't the Political Officer said it was "our sworn duty to help win independence for our brothers in the South"? Hadn't he said to be patient, that the enemy was fighting among themselves and growing tired of the war and would go home soon? Yes, . . . the Imperialists would quit as he had promised. It was hard to understand or believe why they would quit and go home when they had all the advantages. Though, understandably, they might be sick of these damn Southerners and just go home. Why should the Marines want to die for them? Nguyen did not understand.

The fighting continued for a time, then a plane began to circle above them dropping out even larger flares that seemed to hang forever in the sky.

How can we ever make it back? he thought. *We can't wait here much longer or the helicopters and bombers will come.* "Shoot the B-40s now," he muttered. "Shoot them now. It's the only way out. We must go now Lieutenant! Shoot! Shoot!"

9

CHRISTOPHER AWOKE TO A shadow crossing the moon. It was almost a full moon, but it was obscured by a rain cloud sweeping past like an old man's beard blowing in the night wind. This was the first he had seen of the moon tonight; it had not been there before. *Must have just risen, or been hidden in the monsoon mist,* he surmised. It made him think of Pappy, though he never had a beard that he knew of; he thought about him anyway. He had never known him, dying like he did before Christopher was born, but he had heard Conrad talk about him so much that he felt close to him, like he had known him himself, and the stories he heard were as if Pappy had told them personally. They were hunting tales, and farming tales, and family tales, like the ones Pappy told about his Pappy and his Grandpappy Bill. One of the best was about Great-Great-Grand-Pappy Bill getting himself shot at Devil's Den with the 44th Alabama after the war. Christopher couldn't remember the county but Pappy knew because it was where they moved from to come farther west. Conrad said the yarns had gotten stretched a bit, but Christopher thought of them tonight as he looked at the moon with the beard blowing towards home, and he didn't have anybody around who would appreciate a good stretched story about the South.

Devil's Den they would understand, and indeed, did understand, but this would be hard for those folks to square, he decided, as the twin engine plane circled above dropping more basketball flares that hung from the ceiling of the sky like huge chandeliers. Round and round it went, blinking its red and green lights, while the chandeliers swung their way down creating long, mournful shadows that glided ghostlike over the earth.

More machine guns and mortars fired in the valley. *Getting worse, but at least the rain has stopped,* he thought.

The moon disappeared.

Raising his binoculars again he moved to the edge of the bunker and swept the horizon in a long, slow movement. Illumination was everywhere. Ring after ring of white phosphorous circles hung in halos in the thick ground fog. The steady rumble of artillery fire rolled in the distance like the thunder of an unseen summer storm. Christopher focused the binoculars in the direction of OP Falcon, but all he could make out was the outline of a large black presence on the valley floor.

Occasionally a helicopter darted down and quickly pulled upward again like a frightened bird.

Delta Battery suddenly fired for effect, from inside the Battalion wire. After a short pause, a *carump, carump, carump,* answered as the rounds landed again. Another helicopter flew over Falcon. A 106 recoiless suddenly fired. A B-40 rocket.The helicopter flew off; the 106 exploded; and the B-40 detonated inside Fox Company's wire. Only the basketball illumination remained.

A pop-up flare shot out over the wire; the laughing and talking had ceased; Christopher felt the silent tension growing along the bunker and holes of the Battalion front. Delta Battery fired again; more *carump,carump* in the distance. Then more B-40 and 106 fire.

Christopher put on his helmet and laid his M-16 rifle over the sandbagged parapet. Automatically, he checked the clip to make certain that it was properly seated, adjusted his flak jacket and reached for the phone.

"Hey, did y'all ever get a report from Regiment?" he asked after ringing up Captain Stoner at the Command Bunker.

"Yeah, the shit is hitting the fan everywhere," said Stoner. "Regiment is getting mortared, and Fox said they got boo-coo gooks in the wire and the AVRN Compound is catching it."

"I'm not surprised. Fox Company is really getting into one hell of a fight next door; it's really heating up. B-40s, everything."

"That's what we hear."

"Looks for real. B-40 rocket just impacted over there."

"Regiment reports that Fox is in contact with a reinforced company, but I don't think they fucking know how many there are out there."

"NVA, huh?"

"Yeah, got to be NVA and more than a company. Fox has got all they can handle for one morning, I tell you that," said Stoner.

"Any chance to get them some more help?"

"Well, things are stretched pretty damn thin with contact all over like it is."

"No doubt they'll be lobbing some rockets in on the air strip soon," said Christopher.

"Yeah, Arty is shooting like hell at the rocket-belt, but that ain't gonna stop em, you know that. Couple of our ambushes got their asses handed to em out there last night; really bad, too; took some KIA's over by the bridge. You know, routine for a month, then boom."

"Right. I'm afraid there're going to be some more before this day is over. Gooners act like they mean to stay awhile."

"That's the feeling I get."

"Any word on the React?"

"I think the Ole Man is gonna want you to take your tanks and some grunts on a little stroll into Indian Country as a blocking force; least that's what seems to be in the workings."

"I knew that shit was coming," Christopher said as artillery shells from Delta Battery's 105's exploded on the mountain to the front. "Where? OP Falcon?"

"You got it. Zell and Craig figure that's the way they got in here and that's the ony way out. They want you to head em off at the pass, looks like, before they didi out."

"Hell, yes, that's the way the little bastards get in here; everybody knows that."

"Anyway, that's what it seems they got in mind–a React to Falcon."

"Sounds like fun," said Christopher. "How's Falcon holding out? I've seen choppers over them off and on all night."

"Their assholes are really puckered. They got all kinds of gooks in the wire, have had em for some time, but they keep blowing the little rice shitters away."

"Casualities?"

"Yeah, Priorities too, but we're having a helluva time getting a Medevac in there; the LZ's really hot, shit flying everywhere."

"I've seen em circling, you know, round and round, all night."

"So far, only wounded, thank God. Got one chopper for a load, but we need another in real bad. Airwing don't want to lose a goddamn helicopter, you know how they are about their airplanes."

"Just like the Green Machine–worried about its budget."

"Right."

"Well, it'll be light soon and it's quiet along our wire so far; nothing doing up here."

"Good. Everybody else says the same along the wire."

"Those basketball flares got this place lit up like Christmas though. We're gonna be blind as bat shit when they secure that stuff."

"Sorry, can't be helped, Fox Company said they needed em pretty bad. Gooks almost bought the farm. Sappers got through in one place; they got some people hurt bad. Dead gooks hanging in the wire; a real horror show."

"Really?"

"Just got it over the horn."

"Bad, huh?"

"Yeah. I gotta feeling this thing is gonna get lots worse."

"Looks like it from here."

"Looks like it from everywhere, Shaw."

"I know, but don't be surprised if we start shooting pop-ups after it gets dark again. Our night vision is shot."

"No problem, but I got a hunch those basketballs are gonna be going till light. Anyway, that's what we requested."

"Good, one or the other. When something is firm on the React, pass the word, okay?"

"You bet. I'll let you know."

"And you might suggest to the Colonel, in a polite way, that we're gonna need all the help we can get. Line up a little arty for us, okay?"

"I'll try, Chris."

"Well, let me know."

"Yeah, no doubt he'll want to brief you and Lieutenant Malone himself. This situation's got him worried."

"Right."

"Okay, bye," said Stoner and hung up.

Another basketball flare floated overhead. *Man, I could read a book up here,* Christopher thought to himself as he picked up his M-16 and fingered it idly. The flare hissed out and fell into the wire, its parachute hanging limply down. He lighted another cigarette and leaned back on the sandbags trying to think of something else.

10

THE FRENCH ELEVATOR rattled its way slowly to the second floor lifting Christopher and Monty Poltam to their room in the Hotel Majestic.

"It doesn't like to carry Americans," said Poltam over the whining motor of the lift.

"This is an interesting hotel," said Christopher.

"My favorite. Very old. I understand that it was quite popular with the French."

The short Vietnamese operator smiled obsequiously from behind the controls.

"Paris of the Orient, right?"

"Used to be, but now Saigon is more like the Tiajuana, bustling with soldiers and overpaid civilians."

"Lots of cowboys on bikes."

"Draft dodgers. Hard to explain, isn't it."

"I try not to anymore."

"Everybody's got a Honda or a three-wheeler."

The Vietnamese operator smiled again, stopped the elevator, folded back the door and nodded his head toward their room which was down the hall a few steps.

"Cam on ong," said Poltam, thanking him with a quick tip that was more like a magician's sleight of hand.

"You welcome, sir," came the reply, again punctuated with a nod.

Christopher picked up his bag and followed Poltam out as the Vietnamese descended in his cage to the lobby. Poltam produced the key from the baggy pocket of his white cotton pants and pushed the door open to the room.

"Nice," observed Christopher setting down his one piece of luggage.

It was a spacious living room decorated with semi-antique European furniture. To the left was the bedroom, and to the immediate right a veranda opened over the street that paralleled the Saigon River.

"Marvelous view of Saigon," said Poltam, swinging the veranda door open. A motorcycle raced by as the city's sounds swept through the open door.

Christopher could smell bread and fish mixed with exhaust fumes.

"This really is an interesting city once you get to know it," said Poltam.

"I wish I could stay longer."

"Three days did you say?"

"Yes."

"What is it they say about Rome? 'A week is plenty, a month too long and a year not enough?' Something like that."

"Is that true of Saigon, Monty?"

"Yes, but I think you could say that about all the Orient though; it's full of little surprises," Poltam added walking over to the liquor cabinet and entering it with a small key.

"A drink, maybe?"

"Scotch," said Christopher going into the bedroom with his bag. "And water," he added from the other room.

Poltam mixed two whiskies, set one on the coffee table and walked outside on the veranda. He crossed his legs and leaned against the waist-high railing as he drank slowly the first drink of the evening. An American ship lolled against the quay, nudged gently by the current of the river. The sun was boiling over the roofs as it radiated red and pink in the western sky. Another Honda sped by. Poltam took another drink. He had been with the Embassy now for two years, most of it spent in Saigon, with brief trips into the countryside. He loved it here, though he understood its limitations, and he could not imagine a return to the bureaucratic hum-drum he knew was waiting for him in the States. He and Christopher had been good friends in college, and he was pleased to see him again, though there was that odd embarrassment that one sometimes feels with an old friend after an absence.

"Nice bedroom and a real bath, too," said Christopher emerging onto the veranda with his whiskey.

"This is the suite I always arrange for when I have V.I.P.'s coming in."

"I could have stayed at the base and saved you all this trouble; that would've been luxury enough."

"Anything for you guys in the trenches, right?"

"I appreciate it."

"No sweat, just a little push here and there, and the thing is done. I've been here a while now. I've gotten to know people."

"When did you tell me you're supposed to go back?"

"Soon, but I'm fighting to stay. I can't face the States just now."

Christopher sipped his drink and looked over the street below. He had on his brown "dress uniform," open at the throat, black shoes and ribbons. His narrow "piss cutter" cap was lying on the silk bedspread.

"I feel like an imperialist," said Christopher as he looked at a small market near the quay where a Mama San was haggling over a small pig.

"You see why the French wanted to stay, yes?"

"I guess, but I've never felt that way at DaNang, just here. Must be this posh hotel."

"It is a beautiful country, isn't it?"

"Yes, but the war blinds you to it."

Christopher had always been struck by the beauty of Vietnam; the sunlit rice paddies and picturesque villages squatting beneath westerly mountains guarding the gates to Laos and China.

"It never seems to end, does it? First the French, then the Japanese, then the French again, then us, then they'll fight among themselves, I suppose, after we leave."

"I think they must love war," said Christopher, raising the glass to his lips again and taking a long drink. "I think maybe everybody does."

"They certainly seem good enough at it, don't they?"

"They're good, especially the NVA. They don't seem to mind dying. God knows we sure kill a lot of em."

"The AVRN act like they prefer life to death," laughed Poltam.

Christopher smiled and leaned on the opposite railing. "What do they have you doing these days?"

"I'm an aid officer. Spend Uncle's money."

"Give it to the gooks, huh?"

"Yeah, the gook-relief fund, though we discourage the use of that word, 'gook'."

"You either speak the lingo to the troops or you don't communicate. Anyway, after a time they become gooks to you, too, so it's all the same; there's no difference. We've given up on the hearts and minds, Monty, no more bullshit after you see a few legs blown off. It's just you or them; it's that simple."

"Listen, I understand perfectly."

"The only one that can win the heart and mind of a gook is another gook, and our gooks don't give a damn."

"Some of them do."

"Not enough."

"How's your drink?" said Poltam shifting his weight against the rail uncomfortably.

"Fine."

"What would you like to do tonight?"

"The only fun I've had was at a Korean whorehouse in DaNang, not far from the Stone Elephant. Ever been there?"

"I've never been to I-Corps. Pleiku is as far north as I've been. Most of my work is here is the Delta. We can do better than Korean whorehouses though."

"Round eyes?"

"If you prefer."

"Jesus, a real round eye. They look kinda tall, don't they, and smell sorta of funny? Let's stick with gooks. They don't talk much, and I'm not in the mood to go through all that small-talk-getting-to- know-you crap that you have to do with round eyes. Besides, if I extend, I'll go to Australia on leave; more time for all that then, you know."

"Ever think about Hong Kong?"

"Not really."

"I've always wanted to go there. Maybe we could meet?"

"Everything is a long way off. But let me know if you're able to swing it. I might change my mind about Australia."

"So you're thinking about extending?"

"I don't know yet. It's too soon to tell, but if I'm not too homesick, I might," said Christopher, knowing that he was not going to extend and wondering why he had even mentioned it.

"Going back home after you get out?"

"Sure, at least for a while. Then I think I'll travel for a while. I've always wanted to go to Europe, of course."

"I haven't been back in years."

"Bureaucratic lifer, huh?"

"I can't stand the thought of the States just now, much less going back to the South. I like the Orient. I'm gonna stay here as long as possible, Chris. It's like malaria; you can't get rid of it once it's in the system."

"The South or the Orient?"

"Both, I guess," laughed Poltam. "Though I shall miss this country if I ever have to leave. I've made a lot of friends here; don't know that I'll ever see them again if I leave."

"Why don't you come up and pop some caps with us? We might cure you of this great love affair with Vietnam."

"I don't know how good I'd be at poppin caps, but I would like to come up to that part of Vietnam. Maybe I can find business up there some day."

"It's not so colonial as here," said Christopher. "You don't feel so imperial and privileged. Gooks take care of that."

"Look," said Poltam after a time, draining his glass, "get cleaned up and I'll meet you in the downstairs bar in about two hours, okay? Sound all right?"

"Right," Christopher added following Poltam inside. "I'd like to look around first."

The Mama San loaded her pig into the three-wheeler and drove away as Christopher closed the veranda door.

11

CHRISTOPHER WALKED LEISURELY along admiring the shops that still managed to carry a French flavor. After taking a bath and donning a fresh uniform, he decided to walk rather than lounge over a lonely drink at the hotel. His path took him up Tu Do Street toward the Catholic Cathedral in the center of the city.

As he pushed through the crowds he came upon a quaint park where two Vietnamese girls, ao dias hanging from their narrow hips like brightly-colored loincloths, moved gracefully along. One stroked her long black hair self-consciously as she noticed Christopher's stare. Across the street a bar pulsated an orgasmic beat, raw and raunchy, more from the intuitions of the Mississippi Delta than the Delta of Vietnam. Inside, Christopher could see the neon eye of a juke box where American soldiers watched the bored gyrations of a breastless whore. He thought of the girl with the large breasts on the yellow school bus, wondering where she was now, whatever had become of her. A Mama Sahn squatted unexpectedly at his feet, grinning through teeth that stood aslant, her beetlenut gums like forgotten tombstones. She thrust up one hand in supplication, for what, he did not know or want to discover; he quickly turned away and retreated toward the Cathedral standing alone in the swirling humanity of downtown Saigon. The girls in ao dias disappeared while he weaved hurriedly through pedestrians, motorbikes, jeeps, three-wheelers and small French cars. He hastened past a market in the corner of a plaza in front of the church. Hesitating, and not understanding why, he turned and entered through the gothic doors.

It was cool inside, and people shuffled by in short soft steps echoing through the hollow silence. Christopher sat down in the back, close to a small chapel. He tried to relax. A cough drifted off the ceiling from somewhere; a whisper; a coin struck the floor; incense replaced the exhaust fumes. Murmurs came in a wave from the chapel to the left where a young Vietnamese man was praying to a madonna that stared down at him with arms open, frozen in an expression of permanent empathy.

Christopher felt like a man granted asylum. He sat in silence until a backfire intruded from the outside like a shot.

Vietnam won't go away, he thought looking away from the chapel to the gilted tabernacle on the altar. He glanced at his watch, then closed his eyes, debating whether to continue to the American Embassy or go back to the hotel. He had driven past the Presidential Palace on the way from Tan Son Nhut airport, and he did not wish to see it again, but the Embassy remained an item of curiosity. At least, it had been until now; somehow the sights of Saigon had lost their allure, except for this Cathedral that seemed so restful and calm. *It's difficult to leave here at all*, he thought leaning against the back of the pew.

Catholic Churches are so peaceful. No one really notices you, and it's comfortable and quiet with no tension or push to get something done that eventually will seem absurd. Sometimes I wish I had faith, too. I wish I could believe again. Did I ever? Perhaps. I can't recall relaxing like this since being in Vietnam. Even at night you don't, not really, with your mind always searching for the unusual sound; the incoming instead of the outgoing, the AK-47 instead of the M-16; the pop-up flare, the nervous gook dog that, once he's fed by us, doesn't like the fish-smell of Vietnamese anymore; the rifle bolt going home in the bush where there isn't supposed to be anybody; the pebble can's gentle rattle on a windless night. None of that now, just the quiet echoes of undisturbed faith. It's good, but it's brief. Life is so brief and sad. Time flows. Time; always time. Can I transcend it? Let it flow, don't resist it, but go with it in harmony. Quit fighting it. Time is pain. I must learn not to care, to realize that it doesn't really matter, then there will be no more time, and no more pain. History won't let you forget. My ancestors are watching (like Pappy on the wall), mustn't let them down, can't forget them. Looking backwards on a train. It's like that, always seeing what has been, and never what's to be. I can't change the past, but can I alter its importance? In two days I will have to get on a plane and go back to war. How can I change that?

"It just won't go away," he repeated, returning to the severe Asian sunlight, then walking slowly down a street that swallowed him in a surge of indifferent humanity.

12

"SCOTCH AND WATER," Christopher said to the Vietnamese waiter dressed in a white waist coat.

The hotel bar was in a small room that opened into the lobby near the elevator cage. The waiter brought the drink, and Christopher paid him. He had gone down to the Embassy, taken a few photographs and returned. He picked up the *Portable Faulkner* that he had brought from home, but after his third drink found that he could not read comfortably, so he closed the paperback and sipped the whiskey. He hoped that Poltam would arrive soon since he hated drinking alone without at least the pretense of something to do. He considered going back to his room but he had told Poltam that he would meet him here. They had been the best of friends in college; they drank together, dated together, hunted together and roomed together. For this reason Christopher had opted for an in-country R&R, thinking that if things went well he might later go on leave to Australia, now maybe Hong Kong. He had been quite glad to see Poltam but felt that there was oddly a difference, a self-consciousness between them that was strange and out of place. Christopher had felt this before with old friends but was surprised that he had experienced it with Poltam; they had experienced so much together, and Poltam had a good mind. He touched the ice in his drink with the plastic stirrer marked "Hotel Majestic" as he thought about this problem. Perhaps it was the inevitable result of time and distance, some sort of immutable law of human psychology, but he knew that there were times and people with whom this sense of alienation did not exist at all. He wondered if Poltam felt likewise. Yet he was glad, genuinely glad to see him. *No doubt it is the war and our different perspectives on it, the fact that he's a civilian, and time, I guess, sheer time. What we need is to get drunk together and get caught up,* he thought, taking a sip. His thoughts turned to his parents whom he loved deeply. He had long since decided this was one reason he missed home. Poltam did not really have a family and had been anxious to leave — he was a natural nomad. Christopher felt envious for reasons that were not clear, and knew it was useless to try to change. Since being in Vietnam, he resolved to go home, travel a bit, then return and teach at a local college. It would be difficult to tell Conrad but he vowed to do it.

I must do it, he resolved, sipping the whiskey again.

He remembered once when Conrad had been recuperating from pneumonia and he had come home to see him. He found Conrad asleep, lying in a large double bed surrounded by a room full of Victorian furniture that Elizabeth treasured.

Christopher had stood in the doorway surveying the scene. His father's body was lying in the folds of starched sheets. Christopher stood silently for a time. Conrad was only just fifty but looked suddenly old with the face pale on the white pillow and his breathing slightly labored. It was then that Christopher realized his father would die. That his mother would die. Barrel would die. He would die. It was a fact that he had known and not known. Conrad got well, but Christopher knew, really knew, then, only then, that it would, must, happen. It was one of the first horrors to breach his complacency.

Then, too, he had noticed Conrad's black, laced shoes under the bed. They reminded him of Mississippi. When he had been a child a man had died, a relative, Conrad said, and they had made Christopher walk up to a large, grey house in the country where the old man lay in an open coffin with people walking in small crowds, talking in soft tones, as the man, eyes powdered closed, arms folded, slept in the corner under a picture window through which Christopher saw blue jays fussing in a green tree. He noticed, too, that all men wore black, laced shoes, the ones they wore at church, weddings, and funerals. He did not like these shoes. Indeed, he disliked any laced shoe, and would pick them up and hide them until he got older and forced himself to admit that this was childish. Today, he walked to the bed and picked up the shoes putting them out of sight in the depths of the walk-in closet where he could smell Conrad's clothes in the darkness.

He thought he had become detached from the old man lying in the coffin in his blue suit and what were certainly black, laced shoes, even though the feet were hidden under the closed half-lid. Seeing Conrad, he realized that he wasn't really detached at all and finally understood what Queeny had meant about death's "black sleeve."

Conrad's eyes opened. Christopher crossed from the closet to his side.

"Hello," said Christopher, taking his father's right hand with both of his.

"Why, hello, Son," he said, his face sparkling to life as if by magic.

"You're a tad warm, but the fever doesn't seem too bad," he said moving his left hand to his father's forehead.

"Oh, I'm gonna be fine, Son, in the pink in a few days. Just about over it to tell you the truth. The Doc was here this morning and wants me to stay in bed a while longer and keep taking these damn pills," he said pointing to a pill bottle on the dresser by the bed.

"I would have come much sooner but Mother said you weren't really in any danger and I had to..."

"Oh, I know, but I'm glad you could get here for a few days. How are things? How's school? Are you enjoying this semester?"

"Fine, fine, exams are far enough off that it won't hurt to be gone. I've got some great courses so there's not much drudgery."

"That's good. I know that you're glad to have all those requirements behind you."

"Looks like things are running pretty smooth while you're on the mend. I've been checking around on things and I don't think there's anything amiss," said Christopher stroking his father's forehead. Elizabeth had always told him that people heal better when they are touched softly.

"Oh yeah, things are running themselves," said Conrad sitting up.

"Turn on the light," he added, "pull up a chair."

Christopher scooted a chair near the bed and sat down. They began to reminisce.

"I did everything that Pappy wanted to do himself," said Conrad later. "Built the empire he wanted — cotton, land, money, even a little bit of politics thrown in on the side, more like a hobby. I only wish he had lived to see it. It would have meant a lot to him, sure would have. Mom didn't see it either, but she could tell I was getting off to a good start. Of course, it didn't mean as much to her. But I did it for them...and myself, and you, and your mother. It's all yours when I'm gone. The really good thing is that you won't have to work on it like I did — you'll have to take care of it, but it'll let you have time to do something else, if you want to."

"Dad, you're a genius with land and money, everybody knows that."

"Well, you've learned it too. Learned it well. You'll be ready when the time comes." He paused, and looked closely at his son. "That is, if you really want it, I mean. Course you ought to do what you want in life, otherwise every day is a misery."

Christopher did not answer.

Conrad pulled himself up higher in the bed. "Hell, son, if you don't want it, sell it. Take care of your momma and sell it or lease it. You don't have to mess with it because of me."

"Gosh, dad, you're talking like Mister Death is hiding under the bed," laughed Christopher.

"Well, it's not too soon to talk about such things."

"I'm proud of you, Dad, you know that."

"Sure, I know that, and I'm proud of you. We both are."

"How are you feeling. Better? Really, better?"

"You should have seen me several days ago. I was sure nuff sick then. Naugh, I'm doing great. Nothing a drink of bourbon wouldn't cure."

"Can't have any?"

"Not while I'm on the pills."

"Jesus, that's terrible."

"You ain't a 'kiddin that's terrible. It's awful."

They sat smiling for a moment. Then there was an awkwardness between them like two dancers slightly out of step.

"You still talking about getting another degree and all that business?"

"Maybe."

Christopher stood up.

"You thirsty?"

"You bet."

Christopher poured ice water from a pitcher on the dresser. "I'm a long way from that with the war on," he said, handing the water to his father.

"They want you to go in right away?" he asked, not drinking.

"Looks like it. Soon as I graduate."

"Well," Conrad said, drinking, then putting the glass back down, "when you're all done with that, do what you want, but this is the richest land in the Arkansas Delta. Just a'waiting for you."

Poltam walked through the door. Christopher noticed that he had on black, laced shoes.

"Scotch," Poltam said to the waiter sitting down and lighting a cigarette. "Get clean?" he asked, offering the package to Christopher, who took one and lighted it, blowing smoke over the liquid, making it fog.

"Thanks. Yeah, I got clean and walked around a while, down to the Cathedral, then over to the Embassy and back. The church is nice."

"Go into the Embassy?"

"Just walked around and took some pictures is all."

"I'll show you around some of it tomorrow. My place is not far from there."

"Great. It looks like a fort, turret-like guard towers, the whole bit."

"It's actually pretty secure in town now, things aren't as jumpy as they used to be. We must be making progress," he added, taking the drink from the waiter.

"Can't tell it up North. We're still fighting over the same sad, forsaken places–Go Noi Island, Arizona, Dodge City, Happy Valley, Charlie Ridge. Farther north it's The Rock Pile, Camp Carrol, Con Tien, Ashau, DMZ, over and over, year after year it seems. Guys on their second, even third tours still fighting on the same turf; kinda like an old football field you play on every year. It never changes."

"Yeah, true, but we're making progress, Chris, little by little."

"I don't see it."

"How long you been here now?"

"Six months."

"Not long enough. It's almost imperceptible, but steady, the progress we're making. If you stay longer, you'll see it, I assure you."

"Guys I talk to who've been here before say the war's changed all right, but they don't see any attempt by the politicians to win it. We just keep fucking around, not winning, not losing, just hoping the gooks'll see the light. Meantime, people keep getting blown away. It's getting harder to explain to the troops, Monty."

"The South Vietnamese are doing better. I see it every day. I can see the big picture that you can't Chris. I know it's tough, but if we have patience, we can come out on top."

"The whole goddamn thing is nuts."

"Look, let me show you around a little, huh? Let's forget the war and have some fun. That's what you want to do, right? That's what you came for?"

"Sure, let's just forget about it," said Christopher, draining his glass. "One more round and dinner?"

"Beautiful," said Poltam catching the waiter's eye.

13

CHRISTOPHER FOLLOWED HIS FRIEND down the half-lit avenue to an even darker side street. Obviously Poltam knew the way as they took a turn into a black alley that wound itself through the urban trails of Saigon. Christopher, following behind, could make out the white coat of Poltam moving ahead self-assuredly like a native gliding through the faint paths of a familiar forest. He heard oriental music mixing with western rock in an incongruous confluence of sounds. A woman laughed, a girl perhaps; it was hard to tell because it was a deep, gutteral, sardonic laugh, filled with pleasure. Christopher stumbled slightly on a stone. The laugh came again, this time with a note of hysteria. They turned a corner and came upon a half-open door emitting a shaft of light cutting through the darkness to Poltam's face, revealing his Latin-like features of straight black hair and slightly olive skin. A Vietnamese man peered out of the door at them and said something to Poltam.

They walked through the bright light into a narrow hallway of tobacco smoke and loud American voices. On the right was a wall of slot machines with people sitting on stools like robots, pulling levers and putting in money. Next to Christopher was a middle-aged American woman, dressed in a low cut cocktail blouse, busily pulling the arm of the machine with her right hand and feeding it with her left.

"Goddamn thief," she mumbled, her puffy face dangling a cigarette from red lips. "This son-of-a-bitch is rigged." She took a swallow of whiskey from a glass perched on a green velvet ledge.

The smoke burned Christopher's eyes as it hung thickly in the room like heavy monsoon clouds. He coughed and rubbed his eyes.

"This way," said Poltam, following the Vietnamese man past the slot machines and up a steep flight of stairs covered with dark red carpet.

He took them around tables filled with Americans and affluent-looking Europeans eating dinner. No one noticed them walk by. Across the room, in a corner, they came to a solitary table under a dim lamp.

"Is this satisfactory, gentlemen?" smiled the Vietnamese.

"Fine," said Poltam tipping him.

"Thank you, sir," pretending surprise. "Your waiter will be here shortly," he added, disappearing behind a group of waiters in white coats standing around a table of journalists.

"Who are these people, Monty?"

"Americans, foreign correspondents and businessmen, et cetera."

"Hard to tell a war is going on."

"It's always that way."

The waiter came over and took their order, fatuously cocking his head back and forth, like a parrot repeating the names of the French dishes.

"Wine?" asked Poltam.

"Sure," answered Christopher.

"Red or white?"

"I don't care."

"Well, red will be better with the meat," said Poltam, ordering a Beaujolais.

The waiter took their menus in one quick motion and disappeared before returning with the two cocktails they had ordered.

"Thanks," said Christopher, taking the glass from the waiter's hand, not waiting for him to set it on the clean tablecloth. The waiter nodded, disappeared again and returned with the appetizers.

Christopher took a tiny fork and forced a snail out of its shell, gave it a touch of salt, dipped it in its sauce, then swallowed it with a bite of hard, buttered French bread.

Christopher surveyed the room and sipped his drink. He had not had a pleasureable meal since his last night in San Francisco before flying to Okinawa. Okinawa had been a three-day blur spent getting in and out of bars and taxi cabs with a couple of other Lieutenants, also on their way South. San Francisco had been another matter, with good food, wine and companionship. Now it all came back to him as the wine mixed with the food. It seemed somehow wrong, though, to sit here enjoying such fine food and drink while a few miles away men were eating, living, and dying in the mud and blood of Vietnam. Somehow it was not fair at all.

"We've lost the war," he announced suddenly, feeling a little drunk.

"What forces you to that conclusion?" answered Poltam, surprised, moving his empty cocktail glass to one side, replacing it with a glass of wine, like a man moving chess pieces on a board.

"It just is, that's all," he added, turning his attention from the escargot and looking directly at Poltam.

"You might give me your reasons," Poltam said toying with his shrimp.

"Well, here we are in this rather garish French restaurant . . ."

"Vietnamese, it's actually Vietnamese," corrected Poltam.

"All right, Vietnamese, it really doesn't matter as far as my point is concerned. This Vietnamese restaurant, where everybody is feeding their fat faces, playing goddamn slot machines, for Christ's sake, like fat fucking pigs, and young Americans are getting killed this instant while we're so damned satisfied with ourselves. That's the point. It doesn't make any sense."

"I'm not sure how to respond to that," Poltam said, after a pause, then added, "This juxtoposition is not only true in every war, it's true in life generally, right?" he added drawing himself up in his padded damask chair and eating a small shrimp.

"Of course, I know, people are being born, dying and everything else as we sit here enjoying ourselves, war or not. But this is Vietnam, not somewhere back in the States, and these people, these Americans act like they don't give a damn," said Christopher, feeling a little silly at hearing his thoughts suddenly put into words. Now it was embarrassing; he wanted to withdraw.

"What do you want them to do? Wear a hairshirt?"

"Yeah, well it wouldn't hurt," Christopher retorted.

"You've just got the bends coming up so fast, man. The war is still too much on your mind. You need to forget about it if you can."

"Don't know if I'll ever do that," he said, "but okay, let's forget it, Monty. Yesterday I'm on a hill somewhere in contact with Charlie, and then suddenly I'm sitting here in a posh restaurant eating great food with an old friend. You're right; I've got the bends, man. It'll take some time, I guess," said Christopher retreating completely and returning to his escargot. He took a drink of Beaujolais, letting it sit in his mouth to mingle with the escargot before swallowing, then eating in silence for a time.

"They care, Chris, but they don't know what to do about it. They just do their job and then come to a nice restaurant to forget their troubles, that's all. It's not any big deal, or an act of disloyalty or anything. You're being too sensitive, really."

"Sure, I understand," he said, wanting to add that he doubted the existence of slot machines in Hanoi, or nice restaurants in the Ashau valley for the troops to forget their troubles after a hard day, but he refrained from saving it despite the scotch and wine. "Let's get this conversation on another subject, like how much I love this bread," he said breaking the long brown loaf with his hands and spreading it over thickly with butter.

"I know the guy that owns this place. He's big in the government," Poltam said after a pause.

"Connections, huh?"

"Yes. It's important that I get to know him and maintain good relations. So you know, I'm working a little when I come here."

"I see," said Christopher, eating the last snail. "Doing your duty."

"Working to help you guys in the field."

"Thanks, it's appreciated," said Christopher, trying not to sound ironic.

"That's why I keep telling my boss that it would be foolish to send me back to the States after I've built up all this credit, so to speak."

The waiter arrived with the entrees, Steak Au Poivre for Christopher and Filet Mignon with Bernaise for Poltam. He took the wine and refilled their glasses. The arrival of the food seemed to lighten the mood as the two began to eat busily and reminisce about their college days together.

After cigars and brandy, the air felt cool to Christopher as they stumbled out of the restaurant and into the street that led to Mimi's Salon.

14

MIMI'S WAS NOT REALLY a salon, but a bar with a labyrinth of back-rooms. Tonight, the clientele consisted of "in country" Americans and Europeans. There were several Vietnamese girls in cocktail dresses seated at the bar.

"Nice whorehouse," said Christopher. They sat down in a booth across the room. "No enlisted types, just very nice, clean girls, right?"

"It's a good place to relax, Chris." Poltam signaled to a girl standing alone at the bar.

"Beautiful women."

"Of course. This is Paulette coming over for our order. What would you like?"

"Port?"

"Sure. What kind?"

"Sandeman?"

"You bet."

"Gentlemen? asked Paulette, smiling. Christopher noticed that there wasn't any beetlenut on her teeth. "How are you this evening? What can I do for you? Brandy for Mr. Poltam?" she said in labored English.

"Yes, I would like brandy, and Mr. Shaw here would like a Sandeman Port."

"Sure thing, Mr. Poltam."

"Everything number one with you tonight, Paulette?"

"Yes, sir, very number one. Business very good."

"Rene been in tonight?"

"Yes, she be here soon."

"Fine."

"One Port and Brandy."

"Yes, thank you."

She nodded and walked back to the bar. Christopher watched her hips move under the tight red fabric. A chunky Vietnamese in a tuxedo took her order.

"Where's Mimi?"

"That's not really her name, but she's rarely here. I've only seen her a few times anywhere. Very rich. Catholic, and her husband is big in the government. The fellow mixing drinks behind the bar runs this place for her. He keeps an eye on things and lets that old Mama Sahn over there sitting in the corner take care of the stable."

"This is sort of an investment, a sideline, right?"

"One of several."

"Like, maybe, the Laotian heroin traffic is where the big money is, am I wrong?"

"Well, don't jump to conclusions. We're working on that Chris, have been for some time but I'm not certain of her connections. I don't think that she's into that. Just the Black Market. That's confirmed."

"Why don't you shut her down?"

"Problem is, see, her husband, like I say, is in the government, real high, and real tight with President Thieu, so that complicates things some." He took a deep drag off his cigarette.

"I see. Makes things delicate."

"Very."

"My, we're really into high cotton, aren't we? Not in town twenty-four hours and already on the trail of the big boys. Don't have to look hard, do we?"

"Not really. It's well known, but it's very difficult for our government to do anything about it. We need them."

"Just need to get in there and win those 'hearts and minds,' Monty. Just get right in there."

"We're making slow progress."

"Any encouraging words for the troops in the field? Anything you want me to take back? Any inspirational thoughts that I can convey about our glorious struggle?"

"You want a cigarette, Chris?"

"Sure."

Poltam handed him one and lighted it. There was a pause.

"All of this is in the line of duty as number two aide officer?"

"Number three. I'm more like number three. Yes, you're right, Chris. This is all part of the job. It helps me if I know where the bodies are buried, so to speak. We try not to waste Uncle Sugar's money."

"I'm glad you all are on top of things," Christopher said, smoking.

Christopher felt that he was beginning to sober up, so he glanced back to Paulette at the bar. She turned around with the drinks perched on a tray and came toward them.

His eyes were adjusted better to the dark, and he studied her face as she approached.

"She's nice," said Poltam.

"Yes."

"Port for the gentleman," she said, placing the glass in front of Christopher.

She touched his knee with her leg as she stood next to him. It was a delicate touch, but deliberate, thought Christopher. He placed a little pressure against her, and she did not move, but seemed to press back slightly.

"Thank you, Paulette," he said, smiling at her. There was a suggestion of Europe in her face. It was angular, not flat.

"You're welcome, Lieutenant."

"Chris. Like in Christopher."

"Anything else for the gentleman?"

"Not now. Maybe later. Thank you."

"Yes, Christopher, I'll be here all night."

"Good. I'm pleased."

"You say Rene will be back soon, is that right, Paulette?"

"Yes, she be back soon. Very soon, Mr.Poltam."

"Good. Thanks." He tipped her liberally.

"Oh, thank you, sir," she said, pretending surprise turning quickly and going to the bar.

"They all have French names?" asked Christopher, watching Paulette's hips again.

"It's good for business. Also easier to remember." Poltam sipped his drink. "They're all very much Vietnamese, but they know that Americans like the French idea so they have French names. You know, it spices things up a bit. Part of the game."

"She looks a little French in the face, and kind of tall for a Vietnamese."

"She could be, of course, there is that strain here, but she probably doesn't know herself. She's unusual. That's why she's able to work here. Nothing but the best at Mimi's."

"Prostitute?"

"Of course."

"I think I'm in love."

"She is nice, isn't she?"

"Who's Rene?"

"I'm in love, too." He exhaled a large volume of smoke and smiled slightly.

"That by the rules?"

"The rules are that you can do as you please, for the most part, as long as you are discreet and good at your work. That's all the government asks and I like it."

"Saigon looks like a good duty station, Monty."

"Beats D.C. As I told you this afternoon, I like it here and would like to stay."

"Funny, I liked Washington. Everybody complains about it and I had nothing but good times there: good restaurants, nice women, and I like the museums. Pretty good theater there too."

"I can't stand the thought of going back. You were just happy to get off the base, anything would have looked good."

Christopher sipped his Port. It was fine, so he took too large a swallow of it intentionally, not wanting to sober up; it bit into his stomach and he was glad.

"This must be confusing sometimes."

"What do you mean?"

"I mean, sometimes it must be difficult to tell the difference between the work-world and the play-world."

"It is. The truth is I work all the time, really."

"When you're with Rene as well, it that work, too?"

"She might be the only exception."

"I'd be careful."

"Why?"

"Well, you never know. Our Battalion cut the trusty Vietnamese barber out of the wire one morning after a sapper attack. He'd been busy squirming his buddies through. God knows how many times he had shaved our Colonel with a straight razor. You know, being patient, waiting for the right moment. Fortunately we had some new people on guard, just 'in country,' and they happened to be awake. Some people felt that he should have cut the Colonel's throat when he had the chance."

"She's okay, hates V.C. . . . ."

"Maybe. Lots do, but you never know. Ball her all you want, but don't turn your back. At least you can look at her face-to-face that way."

"How's your Port?"

"Beats Ham-and-Mothers."

"Hams-and-Mothers?"

"Yeah, ham and eggs, 'C' Rats."

"Your troops have imagination."

"It's the only way."

"We live in different worlds, you know?"

"Vietnam has its own little subdivisions."

"I can see better now. My eyes are adjusting."

"Me too. I'm getting back my night vision."

Music began to play softly from a stereo behind the bar. It was the very best Pioneer equipment, ordered through the PX from Japan. The Japanese were obviously making money on the war. The room had tables in the middle with booths wrapped around the walls. In the corner at the opposite end of the bar, toward the back, was a door painted bright red with an ornate golden dragon spitting fire over the middle panel.

"Lot of discertion being exercised behind the red door, I guess," said Christopher.

Two drunk American civilians laughed loudly in the booth nearby. A satin picture of a matador hung above their heads, glittering in border-town garishness. Above Christopher was a companion portrait of a senorita with large breasts. She smiled coldly. The bullfighter was sweeping a cape in front of a black bull with large testicles, bleeding from the shoulder hump and hooking through a veronica pass.

There was more laughter. One of the Americans kept repeating something over and over, and laughing, talking without listening.

"The girls' rooms are through that door," said Poltam.

"Is Rene back there now?"

"Maybe. It doesn't matter, Chris."

Christopher wondered. Monty was not the first on a long tour to fall in love with a prostitute.

"Well, when it starts mattering, you had better give her up."

"I'm not a such a fool."

"Sure. It's none of my business, of course."

"She's nice to me, that's all."

"I understand. Just don't want you to get it in the back."

"You like Paulette?"

"A little. She available?"

"Perhaps. They don't work the tables unless they are, generally."

"Maybe later. I'm enjoying my Port just now. She's nice though."

"What do you think of going to prostitutes, Chris?"

"I didn't know we had any choice," he answered, after a pause.

"This has been the only place for me. Here in Saigon. Somehow it seems okay here. It's so accepted, not like college when they were passing around some 'dirty leg' in the back seat of a car."

"Okinawa was the first whore for me. I had a nice girl back in San Francisco before I caught the big bird over. She was real fine, a student type, but kept going on and on about the war and why I was wrong and all. You know, the usual crap. I just wanted some companionship, nothing else, no politics. Anyway, when I got to Okinawa I shacked up with this little gook with no tits; none of them have any tits. Of course, I had to pay her. You try to forget about it, but you really can't."

"That was your first real prostitute?"

"Right."

"Does it bother you?"

"Like you say, here it's different. I met some buddies from Basic School and they showed be around. I was coming South, so it didn't matter; nothing matters when you're coming down South, man, nothing. You know, you figure you're gonna die the first goddamn day. It was a couple of weeks later that that almost happened. You guys don't almost die in Saigon, do you?"

"You never know here. You just finished warning me about Rene."

"This is more like a gang war, right?"

"Well, sort of. I get into the countryside though. We drive some and fly a lot in helicopters. Several of our people have been killed like that."

"They're quite serious about the whole thing, using real bullets you know. The whole exercise is definitely live fire."

"We tend to have more illusions here, develop a false sense of security."

"Like back in the World?"

"You anxious to get back, I guess?"

"You might say that. The troops act like it's gonna be like when they were in high school, all funsies, but they're in for a shock."

"There won't be any bands this time, right?"

"Yeah, that, and the fact that they'll have to get a dull goddamn job of some kind, only there won't by many, and when they finally find one they'll hate it and wish they could get back with their ole buddies on liberty somewhere."

"Do you think many will come back in?"

"A few. But they'll be older, and get promoted, and be expected to carry some responsibility; it won't be like the old days; it never is."

"No one gives a shit in the world either."

"Not many."

"You still looking forward to going home, though?"

"Sure. Because it will mean that I survived. I don't want to die here."

"Of course."

"I guess I don't love war enough."

One of the drunks got up and staggered to the bar, said something to Paulette, who shook her head, and leaving her, wobbled through the dragon door, disappearing.

"Do you think men love war, Christopher?"

"Yes, until somebody gets hurt, and that happens rather quickly."

One of the girls came over to Paulette, said something in Vietnamese, and followed through the dragon door.

"Think he can perform with all that booze in him?" said Poltam.

"Who cares?"

"Nobody."

"Not even the whore."

"What about Rene?"

"What about her?"

"Does she care?"

"It's different with us, Chris."

"Sure."

"With others it's just business."

"I understand. The earth moves, right?"

"What?"

"Nothing. It's just for real with the number-three-round-eye-aide-officer."

"She's good to me. That's all I give a damn about."

"I'm sorry, it's none of my business."

"It's okay. We were talking about whores."

"Do you think she went to the fat drunk?"

"The girl that spoke to Paulette?"

"Yeah."

"Sure. I mean it looked that way."

"He didn't even buy her a drink, or anything."

"He comes here all the time; he knows what he wants."

"You know him?"

"Yeah, some kind of newspaper type."

"Propaganda for the gooks."

"Come off it."

"I don't like them, sorry."

"Look, what do you want for him, a firing squad?"

"No, I would just like somebody to be on our side for a change. I guess I'm a little traditional."

"It's complicated."

"Goddamn it, I know that, but I still have kind of a simplistic notion that somebody ought to say something from our point of view, that's all. We have a story, too."

"Let's forget that bullshit. You want another Port?"

"Sure." He drained his glass.

Poltam motioned to Paulette for another round of drinks.

"I miss home, especially the fall of the year. You know, like in late October when the leaves are starting to turn, and it's getting cool. I miss that."

"I haven't thought about it in a long time."

"Do you miss it?"

"Not really, I'm making a new life, a new career, and I try not to think about the things I liked about home."

"You don't miss the woods with the trees on fire and the fog rising off a morning stream full of fish with nobody around and nothing to do all day but hunt or maybe fish, you don't miss that?"

"Sure. But that's behind me."

"I can't think of much else."

"Obviously you're going back. I'm not. I want to get out of the South, so I try not to think about the good things."

"Just the bad."

"The bad I don't have to think about; it thinks for me."

"I understand."

"I like it here."

"Look, when you get over this Graham Greene stuff come home for a visit and we'll take off for the hills."

"Sounds good, but I don't know when it'll be."

"I guess in ten years or so you'll be 'exporter' in Singapore or Hong Kong. A man of mystery who hides his Southern accent behind midwestern tones and has a drink every night with a Vietnamese girl sneaked to safety after the debacle. I can see it now, and all because you don't want to go home."

"I plan to stay with the government."

Paulette arrived with the drinks, touching Christopher's knee again. He thanked and paid her.

"It beats selling insurance in Memphis, huh, Monty?"

"Anything is better than that. That's why men like it here, I guess, because they don't want to do that."

"It's an adventure, until somebody gets hurt, and that happens awfully quick," said Christopher, realizing that he was repeating himself and hoping that Poltam didn't notice.

"You hate war then?"

"Yes, truly. But I'll never be satisfied with peace either; it's strange."

"I think I understand. I wouldn't have if I had never been here."

"No one would." Christopher sipped his Port. Poltam exhaled more smoke.

"It's crazy," said Christopher, to no one in particular. A Vietnamese girl walked through the front door, looked around briefly, and came over.

"Christopher, this is Rene," said Poltam. She sat down and kissed him.

"Hi, Ma'm," said Christopher, laughing.

"Hi, Lieutenant. You friend of Monty?"

74

"Yes. An old friend from back in the World."

"You big friend of mine then."

"Yeah, well, we used to scout the Bayou Blanc bottoms together in the good ole days. Before things got so complicated."

15

CHRISTOPHER LOOKED AT HIS watch; it was 4:45 a.m. and his head hurt. The room was small and dimly lit. The door was a few feet from the end of the narrow bed. He lay still for a moment trying to remember. Yes, it was the third one down on the left after you came through the dragon door. A small lamp burned behind a candle, furnishing the only light from its place on a table next to the wall. There was no window. On the opposite side above the dressing table was a crucifix. The table itself was draped with a white cloth hanging over the edges. On it were an odd assortment of things—cosmetics, cigarettes, a purse, ashtray, hand mirror, empty whiskey glass (he remembered bringing that himself), and a Madonna of plaster standing prayerfully near the burned down candle. The Madonna was about eight inches tall, on a small pedestal, with a bowl of dead flowers to her right. There was a cheap-looking chair that had found its way from the American PX sitting in a half turn in front of the table.

Paulette stirred under his arm. Her hair lay in black folds on the pillow. She stirred restlessly again. Christopher noticed that her false eyelashes were gone, and she looked oddly innocent as she lay naked under the sheet, her hips touching his warmly. She was different from the whore in Okinawa, he thought, as she opened her eyes.

"Hi," said Christopher, leaning over her.

"Good morning, Lieutenant," she smiled.

"Morning."

"You sleep much?"

"Yes, some."

"Bad head?"

"Yes, very bad."

"Boo-coo whiskey, Lieutenant."

"Whiskey number ten."

"Lieutenant have big time."

"How about you?"

"Yes, me too, Lieutenant."

Christopher fumbled for his lighter on the floor. He lit a cigarette, glancing at his uniform that was draped in a wad over the back of the plastic chair.

"Like I said last night, call me Chris, okay?"

"Sure, Chris," she said, reaching for the cigarette, and inhaling deeply.

"Chris, number one American lover."

"You tell em all that."

"You not rough like some."

"I'm glad. You hungry?"

"Sure thing. I need head-call first."

"You go ahead."

She slipped into a robe and disappeared through the door to the restroom at the end of the narrow hallway. Christopher remained in bed smoking, now propped on both pillows. When she returned to the room, she let her robe fall, revealing long slender legs and thighs that were not typical of Vietnamese. Her small, but well formed breasts hung straight down as she crawled on her hands and knees across the sheets.

Christopher grabbed his pants and walked through the door and down the hall to the toilet. He passed several rooms on the way hearing men and women laughing. Standing in the darkness of the lavatory he heard another door open and voices talking and again laughing shrilly. Then the door closed. Music began to play. He opened the toilet door into what now seemed to be a well-lit hall. No one was there. The music was coming from another room, from a radio perhaps. He realized suddenly, strangely, that he knew absolutely no one in this city but Poltam and Paulette. There was a naked bulb burning in the center of the ceiling. It reminded him of what a prison basement must be like in the bowels of some dungeon. How had he wound up in this place? He felt a sense of claustrophobia as he stood at the toilet entrance zipping his pants. Then there was Paulette; he liked her, and he hurried back to the room where she lay naked under the sheets smiling as he rolled over to her warmth.

Poltam had disappeared with Rene. Christopher had ordered another Scotch mist from Paulette before making the contract.

"Sure," she had said. "I turned the fat man down waiting for you, Lieutenant."

"I'm glad," he had said.

"You like Paulette?"

"I love Paulette," he responded, getting a little bit drunker with courage.

"You really turn fat man down for me?" he asked. He pulled her closer with his left hand on her hip.

"You bet, Lieutenant. You my number-one American lover."

"Paulette, number one."

"Lieutenant number one, too."

"Chris, okay?"

"Chris."

"Yes. Lover now, too."

"Yes. Lover now, too, good time, Chris."

Christopher loved her cheap perfume as it hung heavily on her neck and he slipped again into the sweet oblivion of her small body.

16

THE CAFE WAS ON TU DO STREET near the hotel. Despite the traffic, they sat at an outside table drinking coffee after rolls and juice. Christopher had changed uniforms, and Paulette was dressed in a clean ao dai of green and white. Her hair was combed back straight, hanging almost to her belt, and tied in the back with a matching green ribbon.

"Will you see Mr. Poltam today?" she asked.

"I guess. He knows where I'm staying. I have to leave in the morning, and I'm sure he will contact me sometime."

"I know where he live. It's not far from here. He has a very nice place. I've been there many times with my friend Rene. Mr. Poltam big honcho. Have big parties at his place."

"Rene is a good friend of yours?"

"Yes, very good."

"Mr. Poltam likes her very much."

"I know. She something special to him."

"He thinks she is number one."

"Am I special to you, Lieutenant?"

"Chris."

"Yes, Chris. Am I special?"

"Yes," he said, fingering the coffee cup nervously.

"Good. Chris, I love you very much."

"I'm glad." He wished he could see her eyes better behind the large plastic Japanese sunglasses she was wearing.

"When do you leave tomorrow?"

"Early. I have to catch a plane at Tan Son Nhut. I have to be on it."

"No more time?"

"I only had three days. Lucky to get that."

"Go back to Ben Hoa?"

"No, Da Nang."

"No Marines in Ben Hoa?"

"No. The Marines are all up North in 'I' Corps. Da Nang, Hue, and up to the DMZ."

"Very bad up there. Boo-coo V.C. I was there when I was a girl but I don't remember it."

"Really," said Christopher, lighting a cigarette and handing it to her, then lighting another for himself. "Where?"

"My father was from a village outside of Hanoi. Very big Catholic. Came South to get away from V.C. That was a long time ago, and I don't remember it. He spoke with a northern accent, but I lost mine living here in the Delta."

"Where is your village?"

"Not big at all. In the Delta. I come to Saigon when he died. He came South to get away from the war. Now the war here again. War in the Delta, so I come to the city."

"Sorry."

"No reason to be sorry. War just comes, Lieutenant. Someday it will leave again. I still have brothers and sisters in the village, one brother ARVN. Maybe go back someday. Very big Catholic village. My mother dead, too."

"I'm sorry," he repeated, wishing he had not done so.

"No reason to be sorry. It just comes. The monsoon comes and it goes; no reason to be sorry."

Christopher sipped his coffee.

"You want something else to eat?"

"No thank you. Your head still hurt, Lieutenant?"

"It's better."

"Good. Too much good time, huh, Lieutenant?"

"Yes. What would you like to do today, Paulette?"

"Whatever you wish. It's your time."

"Just one day."

"My father said a lifetime could fill up one day."

"It is a nice day, isn't it?"

"Very nice. Sun, but not hot. Very nice."

"The rains will come, but today is nice."

"Yes. We have all day. Don't worry about the rains, Lieutenant. They will take care of themselves."

"I'm glad that I found you last night. I was lucky. Real lucky."

"Thank you, Lieutenant. I'm glad I didn't go out with the fat drunk. He Yie Yae." She laughed.

"Yie Yae?"

"Yes, dirty-ole-man."

"I was drunk, too."

"You a good drunk though, Lieutenant, not a fat-ole-man-drunk."

"Can we have dinner together tonight, Paulette?"

"Sure thing. Today is all yours. All just for you, you only."

"Good. I'm glad."

"I'm very glad you think I'm special."

"You are special. I had a girl in Okinawa but she wasn't special. You are different."

"Thank you very much. Do you have an American girl back home?"

"Yes. Well, I had a girl in San Francisco, a college girl."

"Was she special, Lieutenant?"

"I thought she might have been, but I don't think it'll ever be the same."

"Not same-same?"

"No, not same-same."

"Gone too long?"

"I knew her for a few days, and she lectured me all the time, between the sheets so to speak, about how bad it was for me to come here. She was against the war. Though it was fun, I guess, I don't think I can go back to her now. There'll be too much difference now. Mine is a divided generation, Paulette."

"She work for V.C.?"

"Not really, but it looks that way from here. It's hard to explain. People in America don't understand this war."

"War is war."

"Even if we leave?"

"Of course."

"She wouldn't understand. I'm not sure I do."

"It is sad, isn't it, Lieutenant?"

"Yes."

"Will you see me again. Will you come back to Saigon?"

"Yes, I'll try." He lied. Christopher knew that he would probably never get back to Saigon, but he didn't want to say so.

"Good. I like you, Lieutenant. You not like the others, not like the fat-ole-drunk-man. Not same-same. I like you very much. You come back to Saigon someday and look up Paulette."

"I'll try. I'll try very hard." He managed to hide momentarily behind a cloud of smoke. "Thanks," he added, smoking heavily still.

"Your father alive?"

"Yes."

"What is he?"

"Well, once he was a politician for a short time, but now he is a very successful farmer. At heart he is a soldier."

"Politician?"

"Yes, very much like your Senate. He did that for a while, more like a hobby. He's very rich, but it wasn't always that way. He grew up very poor like a lot of your villagers here in the countryside. His father died just trying to scratch out a living from the soil. Dad was ambitious and ran away to the University to get away. After World War II he came home and made a lot of money farming."

"Very rich? Big honcho?"

"Yes, number one honcho."

"Raise boo-coo rice?"

"Yes, and cotton and now beans, too."

"Boo-coo water buffaloes?

"No, just machines. Don't even use mules anymore."

"No water buffaloes in the United States?"

"No."

"Big soldier, too?"

"Not anymore. But once he was; big hero in the Army at Normandy."

"Where is Normandy?"

"In France."

"Oh, yes. I have relatives in Paris. I would like to go there someday."

"So would I. Maybe we can meet there someday. Saigon reminds me of what I imagine Paris to be like."

"Paris very beautiful, everybody say."

"Yes. I'm sure it must be."

"Is that why you are a soldier, Lieutenant?"

"I'm sorry, I don't understand."

"Because your father was also?"

"Yes. I suppose so. It's bred into you. But really I'm not a soldier, not Army, but I'm a Marine and there's supposed to be a difference."

"Is there a difference?"

"Yes, the Army has more money," laughed Christopher quietly. "But you're right, that's why I'm a soldier, too."

"You wanted to be like your father?"

"Not to have been a soldier in my family would have been a disgrace. It's a long tradition."

"Do you like being a soldier, Lieutenant?"

"Sometimes. There are things I like and things I don't like. What did your father do when he came South?"

"He came to a village and got a job with the government. He did not farm anymore. When my mother died, then he died, and I come to Saigon. No money in the village and I did not want to farm. I like it here. Mimi is good to me very much. Boo-coo money here. I like American soldiers. They are good to me, too."

"I see," said Christopher, playing with his coffee spoon.

"You want to make love now?"

"Sure," said Christopher, surprised.

"You feel better? Head not hurt. We can make love now. I'm not hungry anymore, and we can make love all day if you want. We have dinner tonight, then you take me back to Mimi's okay?"

"Of course."

"Hotel very nice."

Christopher got up and paid the bill and then turned and walked back to her standing in the sunlit street. She put her arm around his waist and snuggled next to him as they walked their way slowly back down Tu Do. They both felt better after the breakfast.

17

THE AIR STIRRED THE HEM of Paulette's dress as she stood on the balcony overlooking the city. Christopher stood beside her.

She's come a long way from a village outside of Hanoi, thought Christopher.

Paulette was oblivious to him. The traffic clogged its way along beneath her feet. They were only three stories high, but this was a tall building for Vietnam, and Paulette raised her hands to the edge of the rail to steady herself as the sun dipped its way into Cambodia. The river swept by, swelling the boats up and down on its turgid surface. A bell clanged lazily somewhere across the river. Then an Army truck moved gruffly past an old man on a bicycle. The sun seemed to brighten, but there was a cloud in the west, and Christopher knew the rains must come again like they did when he first came to Vietnam, all heavy and dark. Yet, it was a beautiful country, full of good rivers, green mountains and trees. A fine country, with fine people, all very tired of war. *Everybody is tired of war but the Communists, and they never seem to get tired*, he thought.

Paulette moved slightly and reached for his hand.

"You are lucky, Chris, very lucky," she said, turning toward him.

"I imagine so, yes."

"You are. You can go to the United States and leave here. I love Vietnam, but I would like to leave soon. Maybe go to United States, maybe go to see my cousins in Paris."

"Vietnam is a beautiful country, Paulette."

"Yes, but too much war."

"War is war, and peace is peace."

"Yes, but I like to go away very much and leave soon."

"I understand."

"You hungry?"

"Yes."

"Let's eat dinner and drink wine, Chris, and make love again."

"Yes."

"You can fill up a lifetime with one day."

"Perhaps."

Christopher took Paulette to Mimi's after midnight. They walked up the back steps to her room, coming in the hall from the alley. He kissed her long and hard and promised to return quickly to Saigon. She seemed a little sad, but happy from the wine and the promise.

The next morning he packed his bag, paid the bill at the front desk to the same Vietnamese who the day before yesterday had operated the elevator, then ordered a taxi to take him immediately to Mimi's. Paulette did not expect him, but he was certain that he would find her asleep. He was not sure what it was that made him go. He did not have time, but he went under some strange compulsion that he did not understand.

The old Mama Sahn met him at the alley door.

"Paulette not here, Lieutenant," she said with a smirk.

"Yes she is. I just left her a few hours ago, and she was very tired."

"She did not sleep much, but had to go."

"Where? Where did she go?"

"Army friend from Ben Hoa. Big honcho Major friend come. She go with him. He number-one-honcho, very special to Paulette. Come boo-coo time, Lieutenant."

Christopher pushed the woman aside and walked quickly to Paulette's room. An American walked past dressed only in boxer shorts, obviously hung over. He brushed past Christopher and went into the toilet where he began to urinate loudly with the door half open. Christopher knocked on Paulette's door. There was silence.

"Paulette," he said in a low voice. There was no answer, so he knocked loudly and spoke through the door. Again, there was nothing, so he tried to open it, but it was locked.

"Paulette gone, Lieutenant," said the woman, now standing behind Christopher staring angrily.

"She gone with Honcho-Major," she added.

He took out the hotel receipt that he had stuffed into his pocket and began to write on the back:

Dear Paulette,

I came by hoping to see you again. You were gone, but I understand. I promised you I would come back to Saigon, but that was a lie. I know that I'll probably never get back here again. I did not want to make you unhappy. Please forgive me. I wanted to buy you a nice gift for your room, but don't have time, so I have left you some money. Buy something nice for me, okay. Something that will remind you of us. Maybe we'll meet in Paris.

Your Special Lieutenant,

Chris

He folded up one hundred dollars worth of piastres and pushed the note and the money under the door.

He turned and walked down the hall.

"Maybe tomorrow, Lieutenant," said the Mama San.

"Fuck you," said Christopher, pushing her away as he made for the door and exited into the street.

The taxi pulled onto Le Loi Street and took a right onto Cong Ly. It followed an American MP jeep for a time, then passed it sharply, just missing an oncoming ARVN truck that honked. On the right, down a few blocks, was the Cathedral, and the Presidential Palace was on the left, but Christopher did not notice. The city was simply a chaotic blur of traffic and people.

He took off his cap putting it on his knee. He felt his cigarettes tight against his breast pocket; he pulled out the package, lighted one, and closed his eyes, holding in the smoke, deliciously burning his lungs. "Sucker," he said letting the smoke out, "You're a real goddamn sucker."

18

CHRISTOPHER STOOD AT THE front gate waiting for the yellow school bus. It was seven o'clock in the morning, and he was sleepy and cold in the December air.

Somehow it seems colder when you have to go to school, he thought as he shivered against the large elm tree that guarded the entrance to the Shaw place. He glanced down the tree-lined driveway at the house, but there was no activity. Conrad had already left to make his rounds, checking his fields before going into town to see his lawyer, Wilbur Webb. Elizabeth was inside, tending to the chores of a routine Tuesday morning.

Christopher turned to the book satchel at his feet. *Damn, I wish that bus would come on,* he thought, dreading its arrival because he dreaded school. It would be fun to swap stories about yesterday's hunt with Randy MacPherson, but, nevertheless, returning to school was drudgery.

"Why do you always have to do what you don't want to do?" he said out loud, picking up a rock and throwing it into the bushes across the gravel road. A rabbit ran out of a patch of brush, zigzagging in terror. *Oh, well, Mom and Queeny said we can have a big hunting feast tonight—rabbit and deer. I can think about that all day,* he mused, watching the cottontail dart safely away into the undergrowth.

Christopher stood aimlessly with his hands in his blue jean pocket. "Mr. Rabbit, Mr. Rabbit, you hear me, Mr. Rabbit?" he yelled. "You sure are lucky getting to lie around all day and not have to be loaded up like a hog and sent into Frenchman's Bluff to be educated, you know that? Nobody gonna hunt you here by this road; you got it made, brother, you sure do. Every day you must laugh your tail off while I have to put up with this learning stuff, huh? I know you do, but I don't blame you. I'd laugh, too," he added as he picked up another rock and threw it into the brush. "I bet Barrel finds a way to slip off and do a little hunting and scouting, too, at least, I hope he does." In frustation he took off his hunting hat, and ran his fingers over his crew cut.

"Sometimes I wish I was just poor and ignorant like Barrel; that way nobody would expect nothing much from me, and I could do just what I wanted to—like try to hunt and fish myself to death."

A sharp noise cracked through the cold, still air. He looked up in time to see the school bus backfire its way around the corner, rushing inexorably toward him. Despite the cold, he wished that it had never come; at least not now – it was much too soon. It was too impersonal, too rigidly indifferent, too much of a separate world that took him away from what he really loved. He felt threatened by it as he prepared to take the slow walk across the road.

The bus came to an abrupt stop. He crossed in a billow of dust toward the blinking red lights. The doors snapped open, and he entered into a pandemonium of voices and clanging machinery. As the bus jerked forward, Christopher lurched and was almost thrown to the floor, saving himself with his free hand as he performed an awkward pirouette into the seat next to Randy MacPherson.

"Jesus, I hate this damn bus," said Christopher to MacPherson who was busy making a spitball out of notebook paper.

"Hey, what's up?" said MacPherson, launching the spitball with a rubber band at a girl's head.

"You missed," said Christopher, adjusting the book satchel under the seat.

"Hell, I hit her."

"You missed."

"No, man. . ."

"You never could shoot."

"Look, she just ignored it."

"You missed; I saw it."

"I'll hit her this time," he said, sending another at the target which was draped with neat black pigtails.

"You missed again."

"Shit."

"Y'all do any good yesterday?"

"My old man got one."

"You?"

"Saw a bunch of durn doe, that's all."

"Your dad get a nice one?"

"Naw, little spike is all. How bout y'all?"

"I didn't get a shot either," Christopher lied. "Dad killed an eight-pointer though, made a great shot," he added, unable to wait for MacPherson to ask.

"Sure nuff? Where?"

"Little clearing near Bayou Blanc Barrel had scouted out."

"No kidding, huh? That Barrel's a good nigger."

"We had to crawl about a hundred yards."

"No dogs?"

"Naw, just Indian-style on our bellies, stalking like."

"Jesus, sounds like fun," said MacPherson, hiding his rubber band in his overall pocket.

"Ole Barrel'll be scouting again today, more than likely."

"He loves to hunt, don't he?"

"Yeah, all three of us do."

"Shit, I can't seem to get the hang of this deer hunting," said MacPherson, looking down at his dirty leather boots.

"You got to know your business all right," Christopher added proudly.

"I like rabbit and squirrel. Seems like there's more action," said MacPherson, belching his breakfast.

The bus left the gravel road and drove onto the paved highway to Frenchman's Bluff. After traveling a short distance, it stopped by a girl standing along the road. She was dressed in a plain blue coat with a yellow ribbon tied neatly in her auburn hair. She was waiting on the other side, and the flag boy dismounted to stop the traffic. Slowly she crossed.

"If that was me, that driver would kick my tail," said MacPherson, scratching a roll of fat.

"She can take all day for all I care," mumbled Christopher quietly. "How old you reckon she is?"

"She's old, bout fourteen, I guess," said MacPherson.

As the doors closed behind her, she walked down the aisle and took her seat nearby. Without a glance at anyone, she took off her coat, revealing a tight blue sweater. Christopher squirmed nervously as he sneaked a sideward glance at the large, developing breasts that pressed against her sweater.

"Oooh, she's growing everyday," he whispered.

"She's too old for you."

"Just a little, couple of years, that's all. Besides, I'm taller."

"She ain't interested in no pups, just ninth graders."

"Maybe she likes horses. I oughta ask her to go for a ride."

"You're crazy."

"She might be; you don't know. I'll ride her on my horse."

"You'll never ride her."

"Sure."

"How?"

"I'll write her a letter."

"What?"

"Write her a letter, you know, a love letter."

"Write her a letter?" MacPherson repeated with a laugh.

"Shut up."

"She'd laugh her head off and tell everybody. Boy, would you look stupid."

"No, she wouldn't. How do you know?"

"Where do you get such dumb ideas, Chris? That really is dumb, real good and dumb. To be so smart, you can sure be dumb sometimes."

"It is not dumb. That's the way they used to do it, like in the olden days."

"The olden days, huh?"

"Yeah, that's the way a knight would handle it, write her a poem or something. Then you could ride her."

"Stupid. A knight? You're really nuts," laughed MacPherson.

"Laugh, if you want, but I just finished reading a book about it, and that's the way it used to be done."

"Books, you are always coming up with some nutty stuff out of books. Your ole man ought to hide all them goddamn books. They'll ruin your mind."

"Why don't you read it yourself, dumb-ass? I'll lend it to you."

"Look, like I've told you before, I don't read nothing less it's some of that shit at school; and I read as little of that as I have to. You can stuff your silly books."

"That stuff at school is junk, and I don't like it either. But I'm talking about really *fun* books; you don't know what you're missing, Randy."

"Listen, she ain't read none of your damn books, and she wouldn't know a love letter if it crawled up her dress. She don't live in no castle, and you ain't no knight coming to the rescue, so just forget it."

"Only football players, huh?"

"Yeah, if you was a football player or a big ninth grader to boot, you'd have a real chance. But you ain't, so you don't."

"And if I was both, it would be a cinch, huh?"

"Then it might be a cinch, maybe, and again maybe not, you can't ever tell about women."

"All right, piss on it," he said as he glanced again at the rising breasts. "Boy, they grow more every day."

"Just trying to keep you from being laughed at; just being a friend, that's all," said Randy as they rode silently for a time.

The cotton fields passed in barren monotony. Christopher almost slept. Then there was a shack – gray, old, returning to the earth. In front was an empty clothesline and a mongrel dog playing with two small children in circles. In back was a fallow garden waiting for spring and an outhouse guarding a woodpile like a sleepy soldier. The house was long with one brick chimney pouring wood smoke in lazy puffs.

They all look the same, thought Christopher.

A black woman in a shabby housecoat walked out. The dog stopped momentarily, looking at her, wagging his tail in confident uncertainty. She said something to the dog, then to the children who, yelling, followed the dog into the house. She was tall, stout, and late in years; her white hair tied with a bright cloth, she was holding a pail in her right arm. It seemed heavy. She disappeared into a tall grove of pecan trees that led to a big house up a long winding road now in front of the window. There were two cars parked near the house, which had two stories, rich and big, with no one in front; now it likewise disappeared into more empty cotton fields waiting to be planted, standing in undulating calmness like a windless sea.

MacPherson said something, but Christopher ignored him. He sat back in his seat. *How silly all that is*, he thought. *The horse, the love letters, and riding-the-girl, how silly. It's all a waste of time. I should be doing something else. I should think of something else; it's a waste of time.*

The bus stopped in front of the school building.

19

CHRISTOPHER SAT SQUIRMING in the back of the classroom. Miss Reedy was lecturing about mathematics, and the room was hot. A steam heater sat in the corner wheezing and rattling as Miss Reedy, a middle-aged spinster, punctuated her lesson with a three-foot wooden ruler advertising C.W. ROOT FUNERAL HOME, giving its name and address in Frenchman's Bluff. C.W. Root was a big man in Frenchman's Bluff and a good friend of Wilbur Webb and Conrad Shaw.

Miss Reedy was middle-aged, drab, with her hair closely cropped. Christopher did not like her, in fact, he hated her, as did everyone else except the School Board.

Mother has taught me to love books and Miss Reedy has taught me to hate school, reflected Christopher, as Miss Reedy paraded back and forth with long masculine strides, the ruler held like a swagger stick.

Elizabeth had encouraged him to read and Christopher wanted to go to college and read more. "That is if I can survive the sixth grade and Miss Reedy," he had replied once.

Where did they get her? he said to himself, watching her like a whipped dog, moving only his eyes, pretending to be interested in the numbers of things. Numbers did not interest him; the adventure books Elizabeth bought interested him, the history books of his father interested him, the outdoor magazines interested him, but the number of apples someone would have left after something else was done to the others did not interest him at all. In fact, he could not understand how it could possibly interest anyone, except someone like Miss Reedy; a person like her could not possibly understand anything that was really important.

I bet that she ain't ever had any sex, thought Christopher. *Neither have I but I got an excuse, at least for a few more years yet.* The girl on the bus came to mind. *Maybe when I'm older.*

Christopher looked in the corner at the sawed-through-the-middle baseball bat that Miss Reedy used as a paddle.

I bet that's why she's so grouchy and loves to use that paddle like she does. She's just horny is all. Barrel says when women get horny they get grouchy.

The heater sputtered. On its top were cartons of free milk given to the school "through the generosity of the great State of Arkansas," according to Miss Reedy. She insisted that it be served warm and drunk by all, a policy that sent waves of nausea throughout the Wattensaw County School District. Christopher could already taste the melted wax in the hot milk. *God,* he thought, *who invented school?*

"Jesus, that stinks," he whispered to Randy MacPherson seated in front of him. "It's beginning to melt already. I can smell it. It's her way of getting back at us."

"It's about to catch on fire," said MacPherson, talking without moving his lips.

"Hey, half the people in this place are going to sleep in this damn heat."

"Yeah, look at Buck Tooth."

Timothy Taylor's head bobbed spasmodically downward. His eyes rolled open as he fought for consciousness. Then he began to submit to the stale air, his eyes closing.

"He's headed down," said MacPherson.

"I'll bet you a nickel that he never touches the desk," said Christopher.

"Hey, look at the drool on those big goddamn teeth of his."

Timothy's head jerked upward in a spastic motion and then slowly relaxed downward nearly touching the desk. His eyes were closed and his pencil fell to the floor. No one picked it up. The saliva collected in small letters carved out years ago as someone's initials.

LC + SW

The saliva curled its way down the crook of the "C" crossing into the "S" by way of a connecting trench seemingly dug just for this purpose by a pocket-knife.

Samantha Williams, maybe, I know a Samantha Williams, she's a short-order cook at the Bus Stop; big and fat with two kids, and big tits. Could be her. Wonder if she married L.C.? I don't know an L.C. Probably don't know either one. She ain't grouchy. L.C. must keep her happy. She's a good cook. Big fat Samantha and L.C.

Suddenly Timothy jerked, bellowed, and kicked his feet in one panicky motion. The class sat stunned. Miss Reedy grabbed the paddle and walked back to the boy.

"And what is the matter here, Timothy Taylor?" she asked in a voice that cracked.

Timothy could not speak.

"Speak up boy. Is this a prank?"

"No'm."

"What is it then?"

"I was dreaming that I was falling into a dark hole, a black hole, and there was no one to catch me. I'm sorry, Miss Reedy."

He bent over the desk, his face in a slight quarter turn toward the class. The paddle was swung into his buttock with a slapping sound. He bit his lip, bringing blood. Miss Reedy wound up again like a batter at the plate. More slapping sound as the bat sunk into his soft flesh. Timothy's eyes were filled with pain and humiliation.

"Now children, it's time for your milk," she announced, standing at attention by the boy.

Samantha ain't grouchy, thought Christopher, wishing he were somewhere else. *Samantha wouldn't do that.*

20

BARREL'S HOUSE WAS A dogtrot cabin. It was bisected by a narrow hall- way and covered with a tin roof. It faced east with two brick, gabled-end chimneys protruding upwards from north and south rooms. Only one story high with a small storage loft, the house's walls were made of oak logs – square, not round – hewn smooth with a "V" notch at the ends and chinked in between with rock-like mortar that made it airtight. The front yard was fenceless with a hard, dirty path leading to a porch supporting four pine columns, and steps which led out of grass dead from the frost. In back, besides the usual privy and garden space, was a well, two log out-buildings, a dog pen, a chicken coop, and a barn, where a pair of mules and milk cow were kept near a quaint pasture. The red Farmall Super-C tractor was parked out front with a wagon load of fence posts hitched behind.

It was January and slightly below freezing. The sun was setting and Christopher hurried down the path towards the cabin. As it was Sunday, Barrel had invited him for dinner, and Christopher was happy for the excuse to get away. He hated Sunday evenings so he was pleased that Barrel had asked him. *Sunday night is depressing,* he thought, pulling his coat tighter around his cold neck and slipping his hands into his side pockets.

He emerged from a small patch of timber. Barrel's house was in a clearing and smoke was rising slowly from the northern chimney into the arctic air.

The sun was orange behind the trees. Ducks would be swirling their way into rice fields in black twists, chattering their way down to the shallow paddy water beyond the treeline. They would settle downward, fly upward again, and then light for the night's feed. A breeze picked up, curling the blue chimney smoke, bending it to the south. *A front is moving in,* Christopher thought, as he caught the unmistakable smell of cooking. The sun slipped out of sight. Grey gave way to black. It was a strange, shadowy kind of winter day, beautiful in its bleakness, crisp, stimulating and slightly melancholy.

The sharp cold cut a raw edge on his cheek, but he did not hurry. *Things are not measured in years*, he thought, *but seasons; not days, but moments*. He paused now in the clearing near the yard. The yellow light form the north window penetrated the darkness and fell in broken shadows at Christopher's feet. A dog moaned from underneath the porch. It was Doc, Barrel's Red-Boned hound, who was about Christopher's age. Doc rattled his collar and trotted out, moaning another official bark, unexcited and obligatory, not like the intense bawling of the chase when his deep voice would echo with authority behind a coon or possum. He nudged Christopher's hand as if checking to see if he knew the password.

"Good dog, Doc, good dog," said Christopher, holding out his hand so Doc would confirm what his eyes seemed to have told him.

The negro shadow of a man crossed the window shade in silhouette and opened the door on the inside of the dogtrot hall.

"That you, Mister Chris?" asked Barrel in a deep voice.

"Uh, huh, just me and Doc. Smells good out here."

Doc returned to his place, disappearing under the porch so he could go back to sleep. The other hounds had to stay in a pen, but Doc had "privileges."

Christopher bounced up the steps and shook Barrel's hand. Barrel stooped a little, his dark face clear in the reflection of the window light.

"Glad you here, we's bout to starve to deaf a'waiting. I hates to jes sit and smell Queeny's cooking without eating none."

"I just wanted to put the sun to bed," said Christopher.

"Ain't it pretty though?"

"Having a cold snap, feels like."

"Yeah, it's getting frigidy with this weather moving in."

Barrel turned and stepped down the hall toward the door. The hall was really a storage area with a passageway through the middle. It had everything Barrel wanted out of the rain: a small rusty washtub, boxes of tools, parts, empty jars, canned goods, old clothes stacked on a chest of drawers, fishing tackle, chain saw, hip boots, work shoes, gasoline can, oil cans, bucket of ashes, empty minnow bucket, paddle, net, five-horse motor, steel traps, and an assortment of mule tack, consisting of reins, collars, and single-trees hanging from nails. The out-buildings had more, but this was what Barrel kept handy.

The light hurt Christopher's eyes as he stepped through the door. Queeny was standing behind an iron wood-burning stove busily stoking it with split pieces of pine. In the center of the room, between the double bed by the wall and the fireplace across the room, was a wooden table covered with a plastic cloth. Its center was adorned with a coal oil lamp that lit the room with a brightness that mingled warmly with the flaming logs of the fire. Barrel had grudgingly consented to some electricity, and there was a Philco radio sitting in a ponderous brown console by his chair next to the fire. He still resisted the installation of a telephone, believing the only beneficial new technology to be the radio, Farmall tractor, and outboard motor.

There was a slight touch of wood smoke hanging in the air mixed with the scent of meat cooking with onions. Christopher took off his hat and hung it next to the door. He was hungry and it was warm here. The walls were neatly paneled with pine, and above a chest of drawers by the radio hung two pictures of their children: one of William, who was in the Army and had on his green uniform, and the other Sadie, in her graduation cap and gown from Jefferson State in Mississippi, where she now lived and taught high school. Above the photographs was a four-tiered gun rack with two shotguns, a .22 and a 30/30 lever-action rifle. To the right of the gun rack was a deer head of eight points, with the ears standing out alertly and the head given a stately three-quarter twist to the left in the direction of the fireplace. This was clearly Barrel's side of the room. Across the way was a repainted bedstand that had a Bible resting on a lace cloth with a cheap picture of the Last Supper above.

Queeny went to Mount Zion Baptist, and Barrel went with her occasionally if he was in from hunting in time. He went hunting every Saturday night during the season, usually coming home late. He hunted with Doc and the other dogs he kept in the pen behind the house. Often, Christopher and Conrad would go with him, but he went frequently by himself, chasing the coon, possum, or fox, whatever the dogs happened to jump first. Christopher loved to go, the three of them following Doc through the frozen bottoms, shimmying over logs, across icy creeks, wading through muddy bogs, briars, and cane breaks after animals that never seemed to run out of tricks. They slogged along dressed more like coal miners than hunters with their head lamps strapped to their caps, carrying only a .22 rifle, matches, compass, and sandwiches. Christopher was always lost after the first plunge into the forest, blindly following these men who seemed to know every slough, creek, river, den tree, levy and logging road in the Bayou Blanc bottoms. It was like stepping off into an abyss, a nether world, whose secret exit was carried by Conrad and Barrel like some sort of charm in their pockets. They were, in Christopher's eyes, magicians of the forest, emerging, after hours of endless turning and twisting, almost supernaturally onto a trail leading to the truck which in turn led to a hot fireplace and bed.

"You ain't been a'visitin since Christmas," spoke up Queeny, poking the fire in the stove.

"Too much damn school work."

"Work?" she asked, turning back to the stove whose smoke vented out a tin pipe and wall thimble.

"Yeah, I hate it."

"Be glad you gots it to hate," she said, stirring the potatoes in a black skillet frying near the meat.

"Yeah I know, but I still hate it."

"I know what the boy means," added Barrel, fixing a cup of coffee for himself and handing one to Christopher as he took his seat opposite him near the fireplace. "I sure didn't take to the little I got."

"You had to work," said Queeny.

"I know, but I still hated it. But glad I went and wish I got mo when I was there. I was lucky though, most black folks didn't get none in them days. I can at leas read and do figures."

"Yeah, but you're smart in other ways, Barrel. You know what they don't teach in school, and that's what I want to learn."

"You stick with them teachers, ain't nothing I know gonna make no real money. You ain't gonna grow up to be no farm hand."

"I wanna live in the woods. I'm not interested in no city life."

"Honey, they ain't gonna be no woods to live in, just big farms and cities the way things is going," Queeny said, wiping her brow with a handkerchief she kept stuffed in her dress pocket. She was a big woman, strong in the arms and hips, fat now, but in her youth she had been slim and beautiful. Christopher could see that in her wedding pictures she kept in her family album. Work, children, and time had made her broad and heavy. This evening she was typically dressed in a cotton dress, apron, and sandals. Barrel had on a clean pair of overalls and a white shirt opened at the neck and polished shoes, as if he had come from church. Barrel's life had been field work and hunting; Queeny's had been family, domestic work, and the church.

"You go to church today?" she asked, shifting her weight and looking over her shoulder at Christopher for the first time eye to eye.

"Yes, ma'm. I hate to admit it, but I did. I hate that worse than school if that's possible."

"You 'n Barrel is cut from the same cloth, just wild Indians is all you two is, don't care nothing about nothing except being wild and free, and doing jes what you want and nothing else. You better get right with the Lord, baby, sho better. Someday you gonna need him, that's for sho. You too young now, I know, ain't got a lick of sense, but someday you'll see, yes, suh, when the ole world be closing in on you, then you'll see for sho. It happen in every life, uh huh, sho does." She began to rock on her heels slightly. "Even ole Barrel Bradford's. Ain't that right Barrel?" Barrel was sullenly quiet. "Uh, huh, *every* life. Sho does," she repeated taking out some potatoes and laying them on a napkin to drain the grease. "You better quit fooling round and find Jesus, that's what you better do. I know you ain't listening, I know that, and if'n you is listening you ain't believing. Can't at yo age. No, but one day, when you gets a little older, and things is beginning to creep in on you, then you'll see, sho will. You'll be laying awake on night all lonesome like in a dark room listening to yo heart beat, not knowing if morning gonna come or not; then you'll know that Queeny be right and that ole heart ain't gonna be beating forever, like you thought it was when you was just a puppy. No suh, ain't gonna beat forever. Sho ain't. You gonna feel the cold breaf of mister deaf saunter up next to yo bed and brush yo face with the sleeve of his black robe; then you'll know what this ole world is really about; then you'll have some sense about things, sho will; then you be ready for Jesus. After that, life ain't nothing but a crisis of faith till you find Jesus."

"Queeny, this boy done had nuff preachin fo one day, don't you reckon?" said Barrel.

"Yes, ma'm, I believe I just as soon have a lickin from Miss Reedy as go to church twice in one day, Queeny."

"Who Miss Reedy?"

"Our schoolteacher. She whipped the dickens out of a poor little kid at school named Timothy Taylor. She did it right after the deer season opened. Really embarrassed him. He wasn't the same for the longest. Didn't come back to school for days, said he was sick, but we knew better, cowed like a stray dog was what he was. She's bad all right, real bad. I'd rather be beat with a black snake whip than have her after me."

"Whippin be all right if'n it done right. Just like raising up a pup, though, got to be careful lest you break his spirit," said Barrel seriously, moving over and punching a log with an iron poker. "Can't raise either without whippin em though."

"You pay attention in school, baby. Then when you gets older and got some sense, you'll understand church, too; they'll both pay off, I promise you," Queeny added, finishing the potatoes.

Barrel held the hot poker in his hand, balancing it like a riding crop, then knocked the ashes off and leaned it against the stone hearth.

Barrel could have been a general if he hadn't been black, thought Christopher watching him handle the poker with authority. *I bet he was a general in Africa once.*

"Seen any turkey this year?" he asked Barrel after they sat in silence for a time watching the fire.

"Some. One big gobbler. Maybe he'll keep till spring, but these duck hunters is hard on em. If'n they'd leave em alone, we'd have plenty for everybody, but folks is greedy."

"Dad said he's taking me this spring to some big club on the river. One of those on a big island."

"You'll get em there fo sho."

A leafless bush blew outside the window, scratching the pane.

"Wonder what the weather be doin," asked Barrel, looking out.

"Snow?" asked Christopher.

"I wouldn't be surprised none. Supposed to do sumpin."

There was silence while the wind blew; the bush scratched the window pane again.

"That durn preachin make it hard to talk," said Barrel, eyeing Queeny who was putting the venison steaks on the table.

"Don't you worry, Barrel Bradford, Miss Lizabeth spects us to hep raise this boy up right, to say nothin bout what the Lord spects. But I figure he done give up on you, so I ain't tryin to save you no mo, jes trying to raise this'n up right and witness for Jesus, that's all."

"You done witnessed nuff fo one night, that's fo sho," he said, moving to the table and sitting down at the head. "Run me rickety."

"Huh, didn't see you at church this mo'nin, too busy trying to assassinate them po creatures to be thinkin bout yo soul."

"My soul'll keep."

"Nex Sunday yo soul gonna keep on the front row of that church, that's fo sho, doin the Lord's business fo a change, uh huh," she said, throwing the meat on the table in front of Barrel for emphasis.

Christopher moved to his place.

"Queeny, you got some more coffee, please?"

"Sure, honey, all you wants."

She poured it out of an ebony pot.

Barrel picked up a piece of steak with his fingers and sniffed it.

"Lord, Barrel, put that steak down. You a dog or something?"

"Tween all this preachin and no eatin I thought I could just smell it first and see if'n it still be good; don't want it to rot none. Hmm, sho smell good, still warm, too; glad somebody assassinated this po creature so we'd have something to eat."

"Preacher sho gonna be glad to see *you* next Sunday. Sho is. He ask me today, 'Barrel dead?' I said naw he ain't dead *yet*, but he will be if'n he ain't here next Sunday with his sorry self cleaned and scrubbed. Sho will be."

"You get this deer, Barrel?" asked Christopher from his place in the middle of the table.

"Naw, not this'n; this is the right hindquarter of that deer yo daddy killed with the three of us las month. The one we eased up on."

"Is he good?"

"We fixin to find out."

"Miss Lizabeth ain't cooked none yet?"

"She put him in the meat locker."

"She too busy to fool with no deer meat," added Queeny sitting at the end and handing a plate of cornbread to Christopher. "Tell her I'll come fix it for her."

Christopher reached for the butter that sat in a large yellow cone scoop on a plastic green plate. He heaped a thick glob on a piece of cornbread and mixed it with a bite of fried steak.

"Boy, this is worth the preachin, Queeny," he mumbled with his mouth full like a chaw of tobacco.

"Ain't nobody can cook like Queeny can," said Barrel. "She starve you to death waitin, a'makin you sit and smell and slobber like a hungry hound, then turn you a loose. I might jes go to church with you nex Sunday fo this here fine eatin."

"If'n you don't, you'll starve fo a week," Queeny said, filling her plate.

The snow fell softly as Christopher walked down the road. It was dark and the flakes tickled his face. The sky was black, the wind raw and piercing, and the footing barely visible. He felt warm inside from the food, but now he felt a little alone and frightened of the two miles he had to cover to get back home. He looked back but the glow of the cabin window had disappeared into the pine trees. "I should have brought a light," he said out loud to the wind. He had lied out of boyish pride and told Barrel that he had one in his pocket. As he stumbled along, hoping his eyes would adjust, he thought about what Queeny had said about life and faith. *But I don't like that preachin stuff*, he told himself, nearly tripping over a stick in the road. A hound moaned somewhere in the distance like a lost ghost trying to find itself. It wasn't Doc. Christopher thought about Queeny some more. It seemed colder.

Now he wasn't sure of his direction. *This is the right road, ain't it?* He wondered if he had missed the north fork, or, perhaps, he had not come to it yet. There was no doubt about it, he was lost.

He looked up at the sky, but all was blackness. He wished he could see just one star, one piece of moon, but there was nothing but pitchy night. More snow stung his eyes and nose as he looked up. There was no light. Isolated, he wished for one of the magicians of the forest to lead him out, but there was none. Conrad had taught him how to read the night sky, but that was no help now. He felt even more alone as the hound bayed again from somewhere in the black wind. His feet were cold, and he felt a chill. *This has got to be the north fork*, he said to himself, standing motionless; but he was not sure.

I wish I was a big red-tailed hawk, no an eagle; then I would fly high above this storm and above the cloud and break through to the stars, bright and clean, just below the Milky Way. I'd sail north to Polaris, then to Orion the Hunter, Mars and Venus, past all the titans of the Universe. I'd fly like a white ray of light into the heavens like a god, free and powerful. He clenched his fist in his coat pocket, but his feet grew colder, and his nose began to run onto his upper lip. The wind ebbed in the trees like waves on a stormy beach. He wiped his nose, but it kept running. *Someday, I'll be like that and I won't need all that damn preachin stuff; I'll be free from that and won't have to listen to it anymore, but right now I've got to backtrack.*

He turned and walked back to Barrel's until he saw the light through the pine trees again. He knew then that he had not missed the fork at all but had simply failed to go far enough. He turned again and walked deliberately, head glued to the ground past where he had been before until he came to the fork in the road, now made barely visible by his night vision and the hint of a moon rising through the mist. It was a dim sliver of a moon; just out of sight, it danced behind the clouds, making its way across the heavens like truth itself.

21

IT WAS 0526 HOURS WHEN THE landline rang again.
"Shaw here," said Christopher.
"The Colonel wants you back in the COC for a briefing on the React," said Captain Stoner.
"Okay, tell him I'm on my way."
"Right."
"Any scoop on it?"
"Looks like two of your tanks and a platoon of grunts."
"That thin, huh?"
"Yeah, that's all they can scrape up. Zell wants to brief you himself; he's worried about coordination, especially with the ARVN–they got the jitters real bad, shooting at every living thing."
"I don't blame em."
"Army advisors have reported contact ever since this little problem started."
"You got to hand it to em, all by their lonesome like that. Like all night, just them, the gooks and Marvin-the-ARVN."
"Yeah, real cozy. ain't it?"
"Tell Zell I'm on my way."
"Right," said Captain Stoner hanging up.
Christopher cocked his M-16 casually over his shoulder and stepped out the back of the bunker into the greying light of early morning.
"Sergeant Love!" he yelled at the bunker nearby.
"Yes, sir," came a voice.
"I'm going over to the Command Bunker to have a little chat with the Colonel about this here stroll they've got all cooked up for us. Watch the fort until I get back, okay?"
"Yes,sir," replied Sergeant Love, stepping out of the rear of his bunker about fifty yards from Christopher. He had no battle gear on and obviously

had been asleep. Brushing some dried mud out of his tangled black hair, he stood near the doorway of his bunker.

"The Colonel wants us to bust some caps, huh, Lieutenant? Mix it up with the gooks? I feel the ole green weenie a'coming."

"Yeah, this offensive must've interrupted the movie or something."

Sergeant Love laughed and scratched his head in mock perplexity. "Hell, Lieutenant, seems to me they're just mad they weren't invited to the club. I never did see a gook that didn't like a good skin flick."

"What we ought to do is take a projector and some flicks instead of a bunch of tanks. Maybe we could patch things up; what do you think?"

"I'm all for it, Lieutenant. Ever since we stopped having those county fairs in the ville, we've had nothing but trouble out there. A good flick and some beer'll get things right again with the locals."

Sergeant Love had been in the field almost continuously since arriving in country. He considered duty back at the Battalion Headquarters to be "skating in the rear." Starting as a Pfc he had been quickly promoted by Christopher till now he was a Sergeant. Soft spoken, experienced, admired by his troops, he was considered to be one of the best Tank Commanders in Vietnam; but now he was "getting short" and simply wanted to finish his tour.

Christopher walked up to Sergeant Love, who lighted a cigarette and relaxed against the sandbagged door. "Looks like a good one in the making, huh, Lieutenant?" he said, taking a deep drag off of the cigarette and handing it to Christopher.

"Yeah, it's not going to be a piece of cake. At least it doesn't look that way," said Christopher, taking another deep puff and returning it to the Sergeant.

"Hell, I'm getting too short for this shit, Lieutenant. I'm tired of playing war. I think we ought to get on line and police up the brass and go the fuck home."

"It's getting old all right. I think Zell is going to want to head em off at the pass or something. Why don't you get the troops together and give them the word while I have this little tete-a-tete with the Ole Man?"

"Yes, sir. Those crazy bastards are hot to go, never get enough. I think they love war, Lieutenant; no shit, I think they really do. They and the goddamn NVA love this shit."

I'll give you the details later," said Christopher as he walked off toward the Command Bunker.

"Right, I'll cook up some ham-and-mothers while you're gone. Hate to see a man fight on an empty stomach," added Love, smoking as he watched his platoon commander walk away.

As Christopher walked toward the meeting with the Battalion commander, he saw a truck being towed through the front gate. It was full of bullet holes and had two flat tires; it obviously had been ambushed during the night. Marines were in a high state of activity all through the compound, dressed in the full battle dress of flak jackets and helmets.

The battalion rear was a small village of hooches – wooden buildings with tin roofs – surrounded by sandbags and trenches huddled together in rows around the Command Bunker, the unit's nerve center. It was perched on a small hill, encircled by barbed wire, mines, bunkers and guard towers every two hundred yards.

This must be the big offensive that's been predicted for so long, he thought.

Suddenly a freight-train sound swooshed and hummed as a series of rockets raced over, heading toward the airstrip. This was quickly followed by another swoosh, and a large explosion shook the compound as one of the rockets fell short into the battalion perimeter. Christopher, lunging to the ground, agonized under a feeling of helplessness as another rocket landed close by. The ground rocked. A secondary explosion shook the LZ, and the base rump-rump of mortars mingled with the clatter of machine gun fire. Around him were confused voices, screams, and yells of "Corpsman up" as a figure crouched over a Marine lying by the smoking rocket crater.

The wounded man was motionless and silent. *It's bad,* thought Christopher, looking at him from behind the cover of his bent elbow. *It's the quiet ones that need help the most,* he said as he turned face down in the mud and debated whether or not to get up and run or remain on the bare earth.

Straining for the sound of more rockets, he jumped up and sprinted to the Command Bunker for the conference with Colonel Zell. More shouts of "Corpsman up" propelled him toward the bunker door that stood gaping out of the ground like the mouth of an open vault.

22

THINGS WERE TENSE WHEN Christopher entered the COC. It was man-made cave, a strange underworld of radios, colored maps, and landline receivers all busily manned by several officers and enlisted men. The activity created a busy atmosphere of controlled chaos. Every radio was being used and every map pondered over as Christopher stood silently trying to catch his breath. Lieutenant Colonel Zell, the Battalion Commander, was involved in conversation with his S-3, the operations officer, Major Herman Craig. Along one wall hung a large map of the Battalion's Area of Operation. It was marked with brightly colored lines – blue, red and yellow – all punctuated with pins of the same colors stuck in the laminated plastic like toys on a gameboard.

Christopher took off his helmet and set down his rifle as he stood un-noticed at the end of the tunnel.

Colonel Zell wore unpolished jungle boots and camouflage fatigues that fit loosely over his fat belly. He was short with dark hair and brown, beady eyes that glared at Major Craig. The Major, tall, athletic and neatly dressed, stared back at his superior. He wore a dusty flak jacket and stood in a posture of semi-attention as he listened.

"What the hell is going on up there?" said Zell, raising his hands over his head in a kind of exaggerated despair.

"Regiment tells us that Fox Company has things under control," replied Craig.

"You mean since we finally got the arty in for them after two hours of screwing around?"

"Yes, sir."

"In other words, Major, we got to nursemaid 2nd Battalion as well as take care of our own goddamn problems, huh? Is that it?"

"It's been a matter of coordination, sir."

"Coordination be damned, I don't want any more of this nursemaid shit. We got our own headaches," he said in a louder voice.

"Well, sir, they·were tied in. . ."

"Forget it. What's the situation out at Nam O and Falcon?"

"The React should go out shortly."

"Good."

"I've sent for Lieutenant Malone and Shaw."

"Where the hell are they?"

"Here, sir," said Christopher, speaking up quietly.

"Oh, why didn't you say so?" said the Colonel. "Where is Malone?"

"He's on his way," said Craig.

"Okay, okay. You understand, don't you, Shaw, what's up?"

"Yes,sir. React to Falcon."

"You got it. It seems that they've got their asses in a crack like most everybody else this morning, and we're gonna try to bail them out, real quick like. You and Malone; it's that simple."

"Yes,sir, I was told that might be in the mill. Two tanks and Malone's platoon of grunts?"

"Right. That ought to be enough. Anyway, that's all we can spare right now; the whole Division is really in the shit."

"Yes, sir, I understand. Been that way since early this morning."

"Where is Malone, damn it?" roared Colonel Zell again at no one in particular.

"I'll check once more, sir," answered Major Craig.

"I want his ass over here and now; I don't want Falcon to buy the farm while we're chit-chatting. And find out about how many casualties we took to the goddamn rocket. Jesus, I wish those gooks could learn to shoot; they keep hitting us instead of the airfield," yelled Zell as he began to pace.

"Find out about Malone," said the Major sternly to a startled Lieutenant standing by a telephone. "And check on any rocket casualties."

"Yes, sir," replied the Lieutenant.

The Lieutenant quickly picked up the phone and began to talk to someone on the other end. "He's on his way, sir. He was checking on the ambushed truck," said the Lieutenant. "The one that got hit coming off of Hill 55."

"What about that damn rocket?" barked Colonel Zell at the Lieutenant, who flinched.

"One KIA, sir, and no wounded," he said.

"Damn it to hell, we ought to lend those gooks an artillery FO so they could hit the fucking airfield; let those Air Force pussys earn their combat pay," said Zell, running his fingers through his hair in frustration. "I do not want any more casualties to these goddamn short rockets, Major. It's embarrassing, like we can't keep our heads down or something. Just walking around like a bunch of goddamn geese."

"Yes, sir," replied Craig.

"What rank was he?"

"Pfc, sir, from motor transport."

"Probably a shitbird. Did he have on a flak jacket and helmet?"

"I dunno, sir," replied the Lieutenant.

"Well, find out. I want to know. I'm sick of people walking around here when we're in contact like they were at some damn picnic back in the World.

I'm tired of this Battalion acting like a mob."

"I'll check, sir," replied the Lieutenant, calling again on the landline.

Lieutenant Andy Malone entered the bunker from the darkness of the tunnel. He was dressed like Christopher with flak jacket and helmet. Slightly shorter than Christopher's six-foot frame, he wore thick glasses that contrasted sharply with his handsome, tanned face and black, almost purple hair.

"What's up?" he asked as he set his M-16 next to Christopher's.

"Where the hell have you been, Malone?" asked Zell before Christopher could reply.

"Checking on the ambushed chow truck, sir."

"We know about the truck. I'm worried about OP Falcon out in the ville right now."

"Yes, sir, just that one of my people was aboard the truck, and I wanted to see that he was taken care of, sir, that's all."

The Lieutenant on the phone whispered something to the Major while Zell was talking to Lieutenant Malone.

"The dead Marine was probably not wearing a flak jacket and helmet, sir, but they're not sure," spoke up Craig. "Corpsman can't say for sure."

"Just as I thought," said Colonel Zell, turning back to Major Craig.

"They said it probably didn't matter anyway, sir; he was so close to the rocket when it hit."

"I don't give a damn. I'll have the ass of the next moron that gets killed without a flak jacket and helmet on," fumed Zell.

"Yes, sir," said Craig blankly.

There was a self-conscious silence as all eyes fixed upon Zell, who started pacing again.

A landline buzzed and was picked up by a Sergeant. "It's Regiment, sir. They want to speak to you," he said speaking to Colonel Zell, who, still pacing, was unaware that all eyes were upon him.

"Yes, Colonel," he said as he picked up the receiver, now assuming a calm demeanor. "Yes, sir, we've got a React going out in a few minutes; things are well in hand."

"Looks like you're gonna lead us in battle," said Christopher, turning to Lieutenant Malone.

"Little trip out to Indian Country, huh?"

"Right. Your platoon and two of my tanks, since that's all I got today."

"Going to take on the NVA battalion that lives in the valley, right?"

"Just a stroll, man, just a sweet little stroll into the ville," said Christopher.

"This is un-fucking-believable," said Malone, "I got two weeks left in-country, and the place blows up. The goddamn country is crawling with gooks; everybody's in the shit, seems like."

"You short-timers have a bad attitude."

"How much time you got left?"

"A whole month, a whole entire month – a lifetime, man, a lifetime."

"It doesn't matter. With this offensive kicking off, we might as well have a year; that's no shit. Lots of tours going to end today, Chris."

"Yeah, for sure."

"What's the plan for the little stroll?"

"I don't have the details, but it's gotta be up the road and through the ville, across the rice paddy and into the trees, cause that's the only way up to Falcon, man, the only fucking way."

"Yeah, I've been out there. The rice paddy's the problem; if we get across there, it should be a piece of cake up to Falcon. Has the road been swept?"

"Don't know, but I doubt it with all that heat flying around."

"You know that bastard's hot. The gooks know we got to come in that way; there ain't any other way without choppers."

"We're gonna need some luck to the tree line. That's where it's at, the goddamn tree line."

"After that, I can flank your tanks off the road, right?"

"We can get off the road once we're across the paddy."

"No way through the paddy, huh?"

"No, man, we'd get stuck. We got to stay on the road through the paddy; it's the only way."

"And the gooks know it, of course."

"Of course."

"Gentlemen," said Craig, turning his attention from the Colonel's phone converstion and walking over to a map, "here is the objective." He pointed to a circle on the map marked Nam O.

Christopher and Andy walked over to him and stood side by side, while the Major briefed them in a stiff parade-ground manner, gesturing with a pointer.

"The situation is this: we are engaged in a major enemy offensive through-out the Division. Our Battalion is in contact throughout the area. Your concern is more specific, and you, therefore, have but two missions, two considerations. The first is to relieve Nam O ville and OP Falcon. As you know, they both have been in contact all night, and Falcon reports that they still have very significant contact. Your relief to them is of paramount importance. Second, you must act as a blocking force for Hotel Company who will be sweeping toward you down the valley. The enemy must stand and fight or attempt to escape through this area between Falcon and Nam O village; your mission is to block their escape at that junction. We anticipate that we will then bring to bear artillery and air support and thereby destroy the enemy when he is caught in the vise between you and Hotel Company."

Christopher stirred uneasily. "Sir?" he asked.

"Yes, Lieutenant."

"Has that road been swept for mines between the ville and the tree line?"

"Engineers report that it has not been since yesterday, too much activity in the area. However, we are hopeful that the civic action unit in the village kept it under observation and fire during the night. We think you'll be alright on that score."

"Why don't we call em up and ask em about it?"

"We have lost contact with them momentarily, Lieutenant. It comes and goes."

"So we don't know exactly what the situation is in the ville at the moment, is that it, sir?"

"We had radio contact with them a few minutes ago, and they assure us that they can hang on okay. But the pucker-factor is high out there, and they need relief."

"Yes, sir," Christopher said.

"Anyway, it doesn't matter. We've got to send the React in any case," Major Craig added. "We have no choice."

"What's the estimated gook strength in the area?" asked Malone.

"We're not sure. The Division is in contact through the area, but our best estimate is that we're dealing with a Battalion, more or less. However, they're spread out thin, trying to fight everywhere."

"Any chance for some more muscle, Major?" Malone asked.

"Your platoon, supported by tanks, ought to be enough, Lieutenant Malone. This Battalion is spread pretty thin; this is all we can let you have. Of course, you'll be tied in with Falcon and the CAC unit, and we'll get you some arty if it's available. Gentlemen, the Colonel and I have the greatest confidence in your carrying out this mission in a professional manner," said the Major, stiffening. "No doubt the enemy is scattered and riddled with casualties; all you have to do is hold them at bay until Hotel catches up; then we'll let air and artillery support finish the job."

"Delta Battery will provide an FO?" asked Malone.

"Right, but you'll be on low priority until the blocking force is set. Delta Battery has been fully committed since this thing started. Besides, we're giving you two tanks, and that's all we can muster. But you'll get arty if it's clear."

"Yes, sir," answered Malone, shifting his weight slightly, like a boxer keeping his balance.

"It is now 0614 hours," he said looking at his watch. "I want you to move out by 0630 and be in Nam O by 0645, no later. Monitor the Battalion frequency at all times, and casualties will go out of Falcon by chopper. Anything else?"

There was silence.

"Outstanding. Good luck, gentlemen, I know you are proud," said Major Craig, standing erect, almost at attention. He extended his hand, which they shook without enthusiasm. As they turned to go, Colonel Zell put down the landline receiver.

"Those pencil dicks at Regiment are in a goddamn panic," he said loudly to no one in particular. "Even they've had gooks in the wire, and they're scared shitless."

"The React is going out at 0630," spoke up Craig quietly.

"Good. Inform Falcon."

"They're told, sir."

"You can't be there soon enough," he said, turning to Shaw and Malone who had not yet made it to the exit. "I want you to haul-ass down there and kill some gooks," he said feverishly, grinding his right fist into the palm of his left hand. "War is our business."

And business is good, thought Christopher sardonically.

Zell was like so many officers whose youthful dreams of glory had finally faded to the faint, bitter hope for merely the next and obviously final promotion. The next promotion. It was the splinter that he clung to, the last piece of flotsam that held his ego afloat above the inexorable fact of retirement, obscurity and oblivion. And today it was this offensive that threatened to ruin even this small consolation.

"Keep your casualties down though," Zell said after a second. "You know how Division hates casualties; keep them down to a minimum. Goddamn it, I don't want any fucking investigations. You understand?"

"Yes, sir," they both responded simultaneously as they turned and walked out of the bunker.

"Good luck," added Zell behind them, but they pretended not to hear as they walked up from the darkness of the passageway into the early light.

"Life's a shit sandwich, isn't it, Andy?"

"Yeah, and every day is another bite," added Malone with a wry smile. "Zell's a real prince, isn't he?" he added.

"Fuck him," said Christopher, not smiling.

"Guess we should've gone to Canada with the rest of em, huh, Christopher?" Malone said after a pause..

"Southern boys don't go to Canada, you know that," said Christopher turning away.

"Yeah, I guess I forgot," said Malone with a slight sigh. "But it's days like this that make me wish I'd gone, I tell you that," he added.

There was more fighting on the mountain, and they both watched it for a time without speaking.

"War's an illness," said Malone, not looking at Christopher, but still watching the fighting.

"No, it isn't," said Christopher.

"What is it then?" asked Malone, turning to his friend.

"It's a symptom."

23

CHRISTOPHER JOGGED BACK TO HIS hooch that he shared with three other Lieutenants. It was a tin roofed shack protected by sandbags. He walked in and sat down on his cot.

Suzie, Christopher's Vietnamese "house-mouse," was squatting over a small basin where she was washing officer's underwear. She was dressed in black pajama pants and a loose-fitting white cotton shirt that had gotten to the street markets from the commissary system. She wore rubber shower shoes on her dirty, brown feet, and her head was covered with a conical straw hat that looked like a wide-based teepee. She shifted her feet under her slight frame and smiled at Christopher.

"Morning, Suzie," he said taking off his flak jacket and helmet.

"Chao ong, honcho," she said, grinning through her black beetlenut stained teeth.

"Chao ba," he replied.

"Boo-coo V.C. today," she grinned.

"Yeah, Suzie, boo-coo V.C."

"Marine bac bac V.C., huh, honcho?" she said as she produced a Salem cigarette, lighted it, and bathed the beetlenut in smoky menthol.

"Yeah, Marine bac bac boo-coo V.C. today, Suzie," he replied without enthusiasm.

"V.C. number ten. Marine number one," she grinned, shifting the weight on her loins.

He got up, took off his dirty clothes and washed his face in the pan of water Suzie kept in the hooch for the officers she served.

"Suzie," he said firmly, but politely.

"Yes, honcho."

"Where are my clean utilities?"

Without speaking she got up and went outside and came back with a clean pair of camouflage pants and shirt. Machine gun fire rattled in the distance as she handed them to him.

"Here, honcho."

"Thanks Suzie. Good girl."

"Marine number one," she said again, smiling broadly and exhaling through the beetlenut.

Christopher looked at his watch. It was 0619.

"Suzie, I'm tired of these dirty goddamn utilities, and I'm going to change," he said as much to himself as to her. Christopher quickly put on the clean green undershirt and starchless, camouflage dungarees.

Suzie squatted back down in the rear of the hooch and started polishing boots.

Christopher laced up his jungle boots, bloused his trousers in a neat cuff above the ankle and stood up before a small mirror to adjust the silver bars on his collar.

"Suzie?" he said, still looking into the mirror.

"Huh, Lieutenant?" she answered, brushing a pair of boots.

"Do you agree with Faulkner that there comes a time in every Southern boy's life, in his imagination at least, that he stands there with them, with his ancestors in the grey line in Pennsylvania?"

"Lieutenant number one honcho," she smiled, still buffing the boot with a shoe brush.

"Suzie number one house-mouse," he laughed. He reached into an open C-ration box, picked out a five-pack of Salems which lay next to the small roll of toilet paper, and handed them to her.

"Suzie likes Salems, huh?"

"Salems number one," she laughed as the package appeared. "Thanks, Lieutenant," she added, setting one boot down and picking up another.

Delta Battery could be heard firing rapidly in the background, but neither of them paid any attention.

"Sometimes I believe that, and sometimes I think it's just bullshit," he said reflectively. "What do you thnk, Suzie?" he said, turning to her.

"Bullshit," she said, exhaling a large column of smoke.

"Bullshit, huh?" he laughed.

"Bullshit," she smiled back, moving her red tongue in a quiet laugh around the deep blackness of beetlenut.

Christopher glanced down at the desk he had fashioned out of used ammunition crates. On top sat some writing material, a few books–a dictionary, the *Portable Faulkner*, a military manual – a cheap windup alarm clock and a burned out candle with hard, melted wax frozen in permanent waves in a C-ration can. Next to it was a picture of Conrad and Elizabeth standing together in front of their white-columned home smiling a frozen we-love-you smile at their only son gone off to war. His mother had on an expensive evening dress with her long black hair just touching her bare shoulders, and his father, standing with his arm around her for gentle support, had donned one of the best conservative blue suits you could find in Memphis. There they stood, posing warmly and sincerely in this very special picture for Christopher.

Christopher sat down at the table and studied the photograph. Next to it he noticed his paperback copy of Faulkner's *The Sound and the Fury*. He flipped to a page that he had marked with his mother's letter. He read slowly a part he had underlined.

JUNE 2, 1910

When the shadow of the sash appeared on the curtains it was between seven and eight o'clock and then I was in time again, hearing the watch. It was Grandfather's and when Father gave it to me he said, Quentin, I give you the mausoleum of all hope and desire; it's excruciatingly apt that you will use it to gain the reducto adsurdum of all human experience which can fit your individual needs no better than it fitted his or his father's. I give it to you not that you may remember time, but that you might forget it now and for a moment and not spend all your breath trying to conquer it. Because no battle is ever won he said. They are not even fought. The field only reveals to man his own folly and despair, and victory is an illusion of philosophers and fools.

"Not even fought"; I wonder if Faulkner really believed that? Well, this war is, that's for sure, he mused, and read the final paragraph.

It was propped against the collar box and I lay listening to it. Hearing it, that is. I don't suppose anybody ever deliberately listens to a watch or a clock. You don't have to. You can be oblivious to the sound for a long while, then in a second of ticking it can create in the mind unbroken the long diminishing parade of time you didn't hear. Like Father said down the long lonely lightrays you might see Jesus walking, like. And the good Saint Francis that said Little Sister Death, that never had a sister.

The letter was still in his hand as he closed the book and placed it back on the table. He folded the letter, put it in his breast pocket, and picked up the photograph of his parents.

Christopher suddenly wished he was home, wished it were over, wished desperately that he could be there standing with them on that native ground. More than any time since he had been away, he wished that he was out of Vietnam, and there at home to worry about the crops with Conrad and Barrel, to look forward to the fall chill, the campfire, and the hunt, there to go to the mountains in the spring and fish quietly in a nearly forgotten stream, letting the solitude and water work their curious magic. There was something mysterious about the fall air on the morning of the hunt and the dawn mist that rose spirit-like off a cold stream disturbed only by the feeding ripple of a trout.

Christopher's thoughts were shattered by the furious shooting of Delta Battery as it fired for effect at some unseen target in the valley. He put down the photograph, which to his surprise was now in his hands, and turned to Suzie who was squatting on her heels polishing jungle boots for Christopher's brother officers.

"What happens if Marine leave Vietnam, Suzie?" he asked, rising to his feet.

"Marine not leave; Marine stay. V.C. come," she said no longer smiling.

"V.C. come; ARVN bac bac V.C.," assured Christopher.

"You shitting me, Lieutenant? ARVN no bac bac V.C.; ARVN number ten," she said earnestly. "ARVN no good, ARVN number ten."

"No sweat, Suzie, Marine number one. Marine stay Vietnam; Marine bac bac boo-coo V.C.," he said picking up his helmet and flak jacket. He strapped on his pistol in a shoulder holster, slipped into the flak jacket and placed the heavy steel helmet on his head. Suzie handed him his M-16, which he rested in the crook of his arm. He reached into his footlocker and handed Suzie two more boxes of C-rations.

"Here," he said.

"Thanks, Lieutenant," she said. "I wash boo-coo utilities."

"No sweat, Suzie."

She stood smiling, holding the boxes stacked in her hands.

"You still think Faulkner bullshit?"

"Bullshit?" she asked.

"No sweat," he laughed. "Time I go," he said pointing to his watch.

"Buddha," she said, grinning.

"Buddha?" he responded in surprise.

"Buddha," she said.

"Why, Buddha?" he asked.

Suzie pointed to his wristwatch with a brown finger, balancing the boxes against her tiny breasts with the other hand.

"Time?" he asked.

"Time, yes, time. Buddha–time no big deal. Buddha say no sweat, Lieutenant," she said and grinned happily. Then Suzie motioned to her mouth with two fingers.

"Eat?" asked Christopher.

"Eat; eat time, Lieutenant," she said and motioned to her mouth again.

"Well, it's time to bac bac boo-coo V.C., " he said as he began to go.

"I wash utilities, Lieutenant."

"No sweat, Suzie."

"Lieutenant number one honcho," she said through a cloud of Salem smoke and beetlenut as Christopher walked out of the hooch to his waiting tanks.

24

CHRISTOPHER WALKED QUICKLY BACK to the tank park where his men were assembled. Here, two 52-ton tanks painted dark green sat side by side. A crew of four – commander, gunner, loader and driver – operated them. They were armed with two machine guns and a 90 mm cannon. Pet names were painted on the barrels; Christopher's was *The Iron Butterfly*, and Sergeant Love's had *Hair* written in a neat yellow script along the gun tube.

These two tanks were only part of Christopher's tank platoon; one was "down" for repairs, and the other two were "attached out" with another unit operating in the Arizona Territory.

Sergeant Love leaned calmly against the front track of his tank smoking a cigarette.

"What's the hot skinny, Lieutenant?" he asked as Christopher walked up to the Marines who were milling around, talking and joking in loud voices.

"Let's get everybody together," he said to Sergeant Love.

"All right, knock off the grab-ass and listen up," he yelled, not moving from his position on the tank tracks.

"Looks like some shit, huh, Lieutenant?" volunteered a red-headed Pfc, sitting on top of Sergeant Love's tank drinking a Dad's Root Beer.

"Gonna take a little stroll, right, Lieutenant?" added another.

"All right, all right, we're taking a little drive out to Falcon. We're gonna bail em out and then set up a blocking force in front of Horrible Hog Company; they'll be sweeping down the valley toward us. We're taking these two tanks and Lieutenant Malone's platoon. Falcon has really been up to their ass in gooks, so we need to get moving."

"Lots of NVA, huh, Lieutenant?" asked the red-head again.

"Yeah, lots. The whole Division has been in contact, not just around here. The little bastards have been everywhere."

"Jesus, sounds like fun," somebody moaned.

Ignoring the remark, Christopher told them the details of the operation. The Marines sat quietly and listened.

After he finished, Harris, a black Lance Corporal, Christopher's loader, spoke up. "I wonder if that ole road has been cleaned coming out the ville?"

"I doubt it. Hopefully, the CAC unit has kept it under illum and fire, but I don't think we can count on it. Once we get to the other side of that paddy, we can get off the road and stay off. All we got to do is make that little stretch from the ville across the paddy into the trees; we'll button up to cross."

"You know there's some heat on that mother fucking road," said Tripper Man, Christopher's black driver. He was from Detroit and said he liked to drive because he "related to machinery."

"Luke the Gook done fixed things," he added. "They got a bodacious mine waiting for our ass, you can believe that shit."

"The grunts will give us flank security up to Falcon. After we get on the other side of the paddy, we should stay a little bit to the front, so we can deliver fire to the right and left, as well as to the front, okay?"

There was silence.

"Stay on the platoon frec, Sergeant Love, and monitor the grunt channel. We'll have arty on call in case the shit really hits the fan; otherwise, it's us and Malone. If one vehicle hits a mine, keep going. Let the Doc take care of any wounded; there'll be a medevac out of Falcon. If your vehicle is knocked out and you aren't wounded, you automatically become a grunt, so bring flak jackets, helmets and rifles in the gypsy rack. Any questions?"

"Yes, sir, I got one," said the red-head.

"What is that, Ski?"

"Is this little show gonna be on T.V.? I want mom to know what a big hero I'm gonna be fighting for the freedom-loving people of South Vietnam."

The platoon laughed nervously.

"Only the grunts get on television, you know that, Ski. No glory for us, just cold turkey, balls to the wall," Christopher said.

"If I get dinged out here, you don't think I'll have any trouble getting it service-connected, do you, Lieutenant?" said Tripper Man scratching his genitals with glee.

"Like my ole lady said before I lef from the World, 'the Green Machine ain't a woman but she sho can take yo man,'" he added. "These little slope heads gonna definitely try and secure our heart beat, Lieutenant. . ."

"Definitely some caps gonna get busted today," echoed Burgey, Christopher's freckle-faced gunner.

"Ain't no V.C., this is N.V. fucking A., man, definitely live fire," Tripper Man added, again adjusting his genitals.

There was another nervous laugh and then silence as all eyes fell upon Christopher.

"Okay, it is now 0624. Mount up and meet me at the front gate. Pull around in front of the grunt trucks and wait for me there."

As Christopher turned and walked to his rendezvous with Andy Malone, the diesel engines started, roaring and accelerating with anticipation. He glanced over his shoulder to see the young men crawling over *Hair* and

The Iron Butterfly checking the oil and track, inspecting their weapons and testing their radios, cooly, almost carefree.

The secret is keeping em busy, and laughing, if you can, he thought as he walked through the muddy tracks to the front gate.

I know, and they know, that out there, somewhere in the bush, or in the village, or around a turn in the road, they are waiting, patiently waiting for us to come, as they know we must, he mused as he quickened his steps towards Malone, who was waiting for him at the compound gate.

25

CHRISTOPHER SAT SWEATING and squirming on the hard, wooden church pew where he was pinned between his parents. The Methodist minister lifted his hands and rocked back on his heels with eyes lifted toward the ceiling of the small one-room country church. It was hot, and many of the members of the congregation fanned themselves with paper fans provided by the local funeral home in Frenchman's Bluff. The preacher wore a plain, baggy blue suit, white shirt, and stiff black tie. As he gathered his thoughts, he would stop, wipe his forehead with a white handkerchief, and drink from a glass of water he kept hidden under the pulpit. Few members of the congregation wore anything but plain, starched working clothes with open collars and loose-fitting necklines. There was no call and response between the minister and the people, as in the black church down the road, just a quiet, disciplined, almost hypnotic attentiveness, in which the speaker was lost within himself, never feeling the reaction of his audience. It seemed to Christopher that sometimes the preacher would seem to forget that anyone else was there at all, and the congregation was nothing more than curious and slightly embarrassed spectators. This was such a time, as the minister stared at the ceiling, totally absorbed in himself, lost in his own world – a prophet searching for inspiration in this hot desolate wilderness near the Bayou Blanc bottoms.

"Christ has a purpose for your life," he said loudly, still gazing at the ceiling. Except for the funeral home fans held in hot moist hands, no one moved or murmured, but all eyes stared blankly ahead. There were no amens or uh huhs, just the quiet steady whomp, whomp of the ceiling fans and the light, desperate buzzing of green bottle flies against a window pane.

"If we would only listen and heed His call," he moaned unctuously, savoring each syllable, still looking blankly at the ceiling, seemingly in a trance.

Christopher squirmed again and looked over his shoulder at Randy Mac-

Pherson who was dead asleep in the pew behind.

Elizabeth pinched Christopher on the leg. "Be still and pay attention," she whispered sternly.

He froze momentarily. He stared at the preacher, hoping this was the end, but it wasn't. *Church is hell in the summer,* he decided. The minister slowly lowered his head and looked directly into the eyes of the people, sitting transfixed. He rocked back slightly on his heels again, steadied himself with his right hand up, palm open to the audience.

"Yes, my friends, we must heed the call," he intoned.

Christopher squirmed again. A dirt dobbler had built a mud nest under the pew in front, and he lifted his polished black and white Sunday shoe up slowly to tap the dry dirt loose. He tapped again, caving in its tiny entrance as a light powder of dust settled on the top of his shoe. Elizabeth grabbed his right thigh tightly, sinking a fingernail almost throught the flesh in the process.

"Christopher," she hissed, "I'm going to cut your water off if you don't behave!"

Christopher grimaced in pain and gave up the assault on the mud house.

The preacher began to recite scripture. ". . .Fear not them which kill the body, but are not able to kill the soul; but rather fear him which is able to destroy both soul and body in hell. Are not two sparrows sold for a farthing? And one of them shall not fall on the ground without your Father. . ."

Christopher looked out the window and began watching a squirrel play in a large oak tree. It was a red fox squirrel. *They seem to spend more time on the ground than grey ones,* he thought. *I wish it would hurry up and be fall. I'm tired of this heat.*

A fat, perspiring lady in front continued to fan herself as the ceiling fan's blades stirred in futility the thick, hot air. Christopher glanced at his father's watch. *Ten more minutes.*

Christopher noticed that the preacher now had his eyes closed tightly, as if he were trying to hide from this audience that sat so quietly during his sweaty oration.

"But the very hairs of your head are numbered. Fear ye not therefore, ye are of more value than any sparrows."

Christopher glanced at the program to make sure that there would only be one hymn after the sermon. Satisfied that the end was near, he slowly moved his hand up to his collar and unbuttoned the shirt at the throat, then loosened his tie.

"Think not that I am come to send peace on earth; I came not to send peace, but a sword. For I am come to set a man at variance against his father, and the daughter against her mother, and the daughter-in-law against her mother-in-law. And a man's foes shall be they of his own household. He that loveth father or mother more than me is not worthy of me; and he that loveth son or daughter more than me is not worthy of me. And he that taketh not his cross, and followeth after me is not worthy of me. He that findeth his life shall lose it; and he that loseth his life for my sake shall find it."

The little fox squirrel ran up the tree and into a hole as the congregation rose to sing the final hymn. Christopher was deeply relieved. *Thank God*, he thought.

The congregation moved in mute confusion toward the door, slowed by the necessity of "visiting" with the preacher who was busy shaking hands.

Christopher broke from Elizabeth's side and sneaked out the back through a raised window. Then he ran around the rear and climbed into the backseat of the Shaw car.

"I just couldn't take it anymore," said Christopher when confronted by Conrad. "I didn't want to do any visiting with that ole preacher."

Conrad drove home and Christopher sulked. His shoes pinched his toes so he took them off. His feet felt good so he took off his socks too and wiggled his toes. Freedom at last. There was silence in the front seat.

"Who made God?" asked Christopher, deciding to break the silence.

Conrad and Elizabeth exchanged glances.

"Well, God always was," answered Elizabeth Shaw after an embarrassed pause.

"Then God created himself, huh?" said Christopher.

"Well, no. He is infinite; he has no beginning and no end, just always was and always will be," she said slowly. "It is a mystery we can't understand."

"I don't think I understand it either," said Christopher. He sat quietly for a while, and then after some reflection, leaned up between his parents.

"God will always be?"

"Yes," said Elizabeth.

"He knows all and sees all, like the sparrow in the scripture the Preacher was talking about?"

"Yes," she said. "But I didn't think you were listening."

"Well, I heard that much," he said folding his arms over the back of the seat.

"Then he knows what is gonna happen to us before it really does, right?" he added, after a pause.

"Yes, that's right."

"An' some folks are going to hell and some to heaven?"

"That's right. If you have faith, you go to heaven."

"Then why not send everybody to start with where they're gonna wind up an not fool around with this life stuff. I mean, he knows where you're going before you start, before you're born, right?"

"Well, you have free will," she said, glancing at Conrad.

"Not if he knows before you're even born that you're going to hell. It would be better if he just cancelled you out."

"Christopher, sit down till we get home. You've asked enough questions," Conrad interrupted.

"I don't think I believe in that hell stuff," said Christopher, leaning back. "That's just to scare people an keep em from hunting on Sunday."

"You're probably right, Son, but you must have faith and keep in tune with your conscience. God will speak to you through an inner voice, if you will listen," added Conrad.

"I been trying real hard, and I ain't heard nothing yet."

"Anything," Elizabeth corrected.

"You know right from wrong, and that's the voice," said Conrad.

"I went outside one night when it was real quiet and tried to listen. I'd pray for a while an stand real still, then pray some more, an I still ain't heard nothin, I mean anything, but a hound running sumpin way back in the Brushy Creek bottoms, so I just gave up and went back in the house. Still ain't heard nothin. Ain't gonna hear nothin either, the way I figure it."

"God has a purpose for your life, Christopher," said Elizabeth quietly. "And don't say ain't."

"But how do I find out what it is? I pray an nothin ever happens; I don't hear any voices or nothin, anything."

"He will show you the way, be patient. He will guide you," she said.

"Well, when I didn't hear any voices that night, I decided I'm definitely not gonna be a preacher or anything like that; I don't think I'm gonna get the call. The Lord musta been busy talking to somebody else, so I decided I was gonna do sumpin else when I grow up. I'll go to Alaska and hide out in the woods, maybe run a trapline or sumpin; if the Lord wants to break down an start talking, he'll have to hunt me."

"Don't be sacreligious, Son," said Elizabeth sternly.

"I wanna be a soldier like Dad was; maybe that's God's purpose for my life."

"God does not want you to be a soldier, Son," she said.

"Why not?" asked Christopher, as Conrad passed a log truck with long bare trees bound in heavy chains.

"He just doesn't," she said.

"Well, he might, you know, Elizabeth, if he fights for a just cause. God might want him to be a warrior for justice," said Conrad as he turned off the paved road on to the quarter mile of graveled road leading home.

"That's right. I'll be a Christian soldier like in the song."

"That's not what they're talking about in that song; that's not what it's about. They're talking about spreading the word of Christ, without whom our lives would be meaningless and absurd."

"Why are our lives meaningless without Christ, Mom?" said Christopher after thinking a moment.

"Because he arose from the dead, and it is that critical fact, the Resurrection, that gives us hope, Christopher. And the song is about the soldiers of Christ spreading the good news of that hope and faith."

"If I am a warrior for justice, will that be all right with God?" he said after another pause.

"Yes, if the cause is just."

"How will I know if it is just or not?"

"Your conscience will tell you, like your father told you, love."

"That's awfully complicated," Christopher said as Conrad drove the car into the yard, slowing down to avoid running over the hounds who ran out to greet them with deep voices. "Don't know if I'll ever figure it out," he said, jumping out the back door and grabbing a Blue-Tick hound around the neck, kissing him on the nose.

26

ANDY MALONE LEANED AGAINST a truck and waited. He took off his helmet and examined the ragged camouflage cover where he had neatly inked a large square which in turn contained three hundred and ninety-five smaller squares. Each of these tiny boxes symbolized one day of his thirteen month tour in Vietnam, and he wondered if he would be able to blot out the remaining fourteen little spots in the corner. Idly he brushed the brown mud off the front to reveal a faded inscription he had printed almost exactly a year ago. It read:

> 1st. Lt. Andrew Malone, 0103429/0302
> 2/5, 0-, Cath.
> Boston, Mass.

He took out his official U.S. Government Pen and wrote in large capital letters: "DON'T SHOOT; I'M SHORT!"

"Here comes the tank, Lieutenant," said a Marine standing in the bed of the truck.

"Chris, over here," he yelled putting his helmet back on.

Christopher broke from a quick walk into a slight jog toward Malone.

"Y'all ready?" he asked.

"You bet. You guys?"

"We'll be along in a second. Just two trucks, huh?"

"Yeah, we'll be a little crowded. I'd like to spread out more but this is all they could scratch up this morning."

"I see you scrounged up some fiftys," said Christopher as he eyed the two machine guns Malone had "sky-mounted" on each truck.

"Might be of some use; it helps to know the supply officer."

"What time you got?"

"0626," said Malone looking down at his watch.

"That's about what I have," said Christopher checking his watch, setting it to conform exactly with Lieutenant Malone's. "0626 Vietnam time and 1626 in the World, Central Standard World time, that is, if I figure it right."

"1626 World Time, huh?"

"Right."

"So, it's about 1726 in Boston, Mass.?"

"On the money."

"Hell, it's in the middle of the goddamn booze hour, man. Just think, those bastards are fighting over their martinis right now in some bar, and we're out here getting ready for this here stroll."

"Weird."

"You bet it's weird, real weird."

"What's the word?"

"Craig sent word to wait till we hear from him before moving out, some kind of big deal with Regiment or something."

"No doubt that'll make us late getting off."

"What the hell, that's why we got Majors running the war, right?"

"Right."

Malone lit a cigarette. "You believe in God, Chris?" he asked, exhaling after a pause.

"Sometimes," Christopher answered, somewhat taken aback. "Why?"

"Just wondering. Sometimes, huh?"

"Yeah, sometimes."

"How about now?"

"I don't know. Reckon God's in Vietnam?"

"Sure, he's everywhere. He's in Vietnam, the cocktail hour in Boston, everywhere, man, everywhere."

"I don't think he's been around much lately; doesn't seem like it anyway."

"It doesn't, does it?"

"No, but I guess I believe today though."

"Why?"

"Safer, I guess," replied Christopher smiling. "My house-mouse believes in Buddha. Somehow Buddha makes more sense here, doesn't it?"

"Maybe, it's all the same thing," said Malone, drawing again on the cigarette. "God's Buddha one minute, and the next minute he's something else, the next minute he's a wandering Jew or something. He seems to play games with us."

"Or a saint or a monk in Vietnam," added Christopher. "Ever notice those monks? Impressive in some ways. To them, it seems the war is just unimportant, something that will just pass away, nothing to really worry about."

"God keeps you guessing, doesn't he? But I got no answers today, fresh out."

"Reckon the Chaplain would know the answers?"

"You figure he believes in God?" mused Lieutenant Malone as he fingered his M-16 trigger nervously, "or is he in it for the benes? The Navy's got good benes."

"I'm convinced he really does, gives me that impression anyway."

"Hell, he's a Protestant. It's just like the Green Machine to get you here without a priest. You're a Protestant, aren't you, Chris?"

"That's what I was raised."

"I forget; all Southerners are Protestant, right?"

"Yeah, almost. I got tired of all that ranting and raving. Y'all don't rant and rave, do you, no hollering?"

"Hey, man how do you rant and rave in Latin?" laughed Malone.

"Listen, rednecks could rant and rave in Greek when it comes to religion."

"Speaking of ranting and raving, Regiment is going to be doing some of that if we don't get the hell out of here most ricky-tick."

"You act like you're in the mood to die for the freedom-loving people of South Vietnam. Just roaring to go, huh?"

"I'm not really up for it myself, if you want to know the truth," answered Malone looking at his cigarette and flipping the ash.

"It's just you and me and some snuffies; that's what it always comes down to in this war, isn't it? Just a bunch of snuffies and a couple of Lieutenants, huh, with the office poges guarding their asses in the rear."

"And a bunch of gooks and a hill, always that. Don't leave out ole Luke the Gook."

"Yeah, that, or a tree line or both; today we got both."

Christopher's tanks were coming. He motioned them around and they passed, belching black smoke and noisily churning up the mud with heavy treads. After passing, they stopped with their engines idling in a powerful rhythm.

"I guess I had better mount up. Call me on the horn when you get the word," he added.

"Right. Should be soon."

"Good luck, Andy."

"See you at the pass, man," he joked as they shook hands.

Christopher turned, walked to his tank and mounted. He waved casually at Tripper Man as he climbed up the front slope plate. Tripper Man's head was just visible through the driver's hatch and he nodded, then roared the engine. Christopher took off his flak jacket and helmet, placing them with his rifle in the gypsy rack behind the turret. A Huey flew overhead as he lowered himself into the tank commander station through the hatchway. He put on his communication helmet, adjusted his goggles, and tested the radio.

"Driver, you read me?" he said over the intercom to Tripper Man.

"Yes, suh, I got you loud and clear," he replied.

He tested the radio with the rest of the crew – the loader and gunner – and then he transmitted a radio check with Lieutenant Malone's radio operator, Corporal Thompson.

Lieutenant Malone's platoon was divided between the two trucks. In full combat gear, they leaned against the sideboards, cursing and joking like boys on a summer outing. In addition to M-16s, grenade launchers, and machine guns, they draped themselves with long, shiny, brass ammunition belts that hung down over their shoulders like scapular badges.

122

It was 0633 hours. The sun was on the horizon. To nobody's surprise, they were getting off late.

Christopher told Tripper Man to stop the engine while they awaited their final orders. Pulling off his helmet he sat idly on the commander's hatch. From here he could hear the banter of the infantry platoon waiting in the truck behind.

"Hey, Hot Tamale, you bring your hot sauce today?" kidded a black machine gunner.

"Yeah, man, you know I can't eat no gook meat without chili peppers, man," replied Gomez, the grenadier.

"There gonna be plenty of heat out in the ville today without needin no chili peppers," added someone.

"Hot Tamale don't go nowheres without his chili peppers, right Hot Tamale?"

"Man, I can't fuck without hot sauce."

"You got red peppers for nuts, huh, Tamale?"

"Hot nuts, hot nuts," he replied, trying to be a sport.

"Hey, Hot Tamale, you be sure and shoot some hot peppers out the end of that ole M-79 today, okay?"

"Hey, man, Hot Tamale is the best mother fucking M-79 dude in the whole entire Marine Corps. He got his shit together, ain't that right, Hot Tamale?" said the machine gunner.

"He definitely got his shit in one bag," someone said from the back.

"His shit ain't in the street when it comes to snoopin and poopin with the blooper."

"He is the best snooper and pooper with the blooper in the whole entire Green Machine, man," added the machine gunner as he pretended to "snoop and poop" behind the wooden side board of the truck. "Hot Tamale just loves to snoop and poop with the bloop," he added.

"Tamale's shit ain't scattered when it comes to poopin and bloopin, right Tamale?"

"You ass holes keep shooting at the Freddo Bandidoes and let Hot Tamale do his thing with the bean shooter, and we'll skate today."

"Tamale. got to do his thing," said the machine gunner, doing a little dance.

"Tamale will do his thing," said another, clapping his hands.

"Charlie got his shit together, but so has Hot Tamale, man."

"Tamale got his shit in one bag."

"Right, Tamale, your shit together?" asked the machine gunner lighting Hot Tamale's cigarette as he fumbled for a match behind the drapes of golden tipped grenades.

"I always keep my shit in one bag, man," he said tapping the wide barrel of his grenade launcher.

'Charlie gonna have his shit in one bag, too, man," he said tapping the wide barrel of his grenade launcher.

"Luke the Gook don't like the Hot Tamale Man with his bag of chili peppers," said the machine gunner.

"Charlie don't like to eat the hot peppers that the Hot Tamale sells him, right Tamale?"

"Definitely," said Hot Tamale, smoking deeply.

Christopher looked at the young sun that pushed its way against the horizon. Through the clouds its reflection shimmered for a moment upon rice paddy water that lay peacefully near a village.

This village, shaded by thick, green trees, squatted in the foreground of the westerly mountains that stood as the exit to the Ho Chi Minh trail. Across those mountains was Laos.

It was beautiful, thought Christopher, as he watched the mirrored light glitter on the surface of the water. One could see these things, he reflected, if one could ignore the endless garbage dumps, pock-marked buildings, trucks, jeeps, tanks, guns, soldiers, barbed wire, helicopters, and sad, dirty faces of children who seemed always to march to the sound of distant guns as they trudged their way along the muddy roads and streets of Vietnam.

If it would just be quiet; if the jets would stop roaring and the guns rattling, the cannons exploding, the radios crackling nonsense and the troops cursing.

How can we ever understand this war? he thought. *I'm still trying to understand the South, the lost cause no longer relevant to anything, yet relevant to everything,* he mused as he double-checked the butterfly trigger on the fifty caliber machine gun mounted in front of his commander's hatch.

Hot Tamale exhaled a large volume of smoke that hung in the heavy, moist air like a white phosphorous cloud.

"It's good to have Lieutenant Malone back; he really knows his shit," he said.

"Lieutenant Boswell got *all* fucked up," someone added.

"I knew that wouldn't last, man. He thought he was John-fucking-Wayne," said the machine gunner. "The Green Machine is flat burning up some Brown Bars, man. Lieutenants is cheap."

"Malone's shit ain't loose," said Hot Tamale. "It's all in one bag."

"Got to get yo bush time up next to Charlie, *then* you can get yo shit together, man. Charlie teach you real quick, or send yo ass home early, one or the other," said the machine gunner flipping his cigarette into the air, then leaning over the rail watching it fall into the wire.

"Bushmaster Six, over," came the call sign over the radio. "Red Dancer, Bushmaster Six," Christopher answered putting on the helmet and pressing the transmission switch on the right side.

"Bushmaster, move out, over."

"Roger, Red Dancer, out."

"Forward and hard right out the gate," he said over the intercom.

"Yes, sir," came the reply from Tripper Man as the tank started, lurched forward, then turned out of the Battalion Compound. A guard sitting in a bunker waved to them as they passed.

Christopher looked behind at Sergeant Love's tank, then the two trucks. He saw Lieutenant Malone leaning over the cab of the lead truck with his radio operator by his side. Christopher felt a surge of power as Tripper Man gained speed on the blacktop. Down in the bowels of the tank, he could make out Burgey's helmet resting behind the gun sights. The loader, Harris, standing out of the hatch on his left, turned toward him, smiled broadly out of his helmet and goggles and said something. He knew it was some sort of friendly joke, so he smiled back and gestured with a thumbs up. Harris returned the gesture as Christopher turned forward and gripped the butterfly trigger of the fifty caliber machine gun.

"God damn it, I love it," he said as Tripper Man shifted into high gear and accelerated. It was 0643.

27

BARREL SHIFTED GEARS ON THE Super-C tractor as it lumbered down the road separating two cotton fields. Christopher stood behind the seat, hanging on to Barrel's overalls while the rusty smokestack belched black soot into the air. The large rubber tires bounced through the dust, leaving it to settle on the cotton leaves. It was August in Arkansas, and nobody could remember when it had rained last.

"Is it wide open?" yelled Christopher over the engine noise into Barrel's ear.

"Yes, suh, it's wide open, Mister Chris. You hang on now," he hollered back.

"I'm on, I'm on. I gotta real good grip, Barrel. Whooooeeee, you really got her rippin. I didn't know this old tractor could go this fast. Boy, we're putting another foot of dust on that cotton."

"Might as well, that shit is burning up anyway."

"Reckon we're gonna have to plow it under?"

"It's tough, but it's gonna have to hurry up and rain, sho nuff. It seems like it ain't rain since las year."

Barrel gripped the wheel tighter as the cotton rows sailed by in one perpendicular blur after another. Christopher tightened his hold on Barrel's tattered overalls. He could feel the half-square of Day's Work chewing tobacco in his friend's pocket.

"Don't be spitting none of that durn chewing tobacco now, Barrel," he said, eyeing the lump in Barrel's cheek.

"I got's to spit, Mister Chris. I'm bout to drown."

"If you got to spit that shit, you holler so I can duck," yelled Christopher as his t-shirt and blue jeans flapped in the heat.

"What say?"

"I said let me know when you're gonna spit that shit!" Christopher hollered again.

"I sho do feel a big ole spit a-comin," said Barrel, puffing up his cheeks.

"Which side?"

"What?"

"Which side you gonna spit on?" said Christopher in desperation.

"Lef," hollered Barrel, turning in that direction as Christopher squatted down and ducked to the right.

"No, right," said Barrel quickly as he turned his head to the right and spit an enormous brown mass of tobacco. It passed over Christopher with just enough elevation to clear his crew-cut.

"Goddamn it, Barrel," moaned Chrisotpher as he felt a drop of moisture touch his scalp. He glanced backward in time to see the tobacco juice swing end over end into dusty oblivion.

"Jesus, I hate that stuff," said Christopher as he looked up like a soldier peering out of a trench.

Barrel wheeled the big tractor down another road that led from the field into the woods where he stopped.

"Reckon we did any good?" asked Barrel, dismounting, brushing his hair and clothes.

"I don't know; those buggers got lots to eat," said Christopher.

The two walked down a small levy overgrown in waist-high grass. Near the pond, the foliage was green and lush despite the lack of rain, and insects hummed and buzzed on either side of the path. With Barrel in front, they walked quietly along through the heavy vegetation. The country around Bayou Blanc bottoms would get cold and even freeze in the winter, but in the summer it was almost tropical. They came to a slough of black, murky water, standing so still that it was difficult to tell which way it flowed. A turtle fell with a flop through green scum and a Blue Heron lumbered into the air. Not paying any attention, Christopher and Barrel moved effortlessly along the creek bank, surrounded by green willow trees, hardwoods, and an occasional cypress supported by gnarled, curling roots twisting from the earth.

"Wonder if that big Cotton Mouf is sunnin hisself in that ole willow today?" asked Barrel as he stopped to wait for Christopher. The edge of the pond was only a few yards away.

"Yeah, and I ran off and forgot the .22," whispered Christopher, as he looked at the willow caressing the water with its lower branches.

The pond was levied for a fish-raising enterprise, long since failed, and it had now been reclaimed by the Bayou Blanc bottoms. The water gave way to dry, cracked mud flats looking like the surface of a dead world lost to the sun. Just visible in the growth of weeds and briars, a rusty feeder pipe stuck stupidly out of the levy, while on the water, insects jerked in spasms across the surface and dragonflies darted about like tiny prehistoric birds. A tick with a white spot on his back tickled Christopher's arm.

"Damn," he muttered, brushing it off in a panic. "I don't know how these bastards live through the winter."

"Shhh," said Barrel.

"Why God made ticks and snakes, I'll never figure out," Christopher muttered to himself as he checked his pants leg.

"Shhh, Mister Chris, let's see if ole Scratch is a'sunning hisself today."

"Hell, you know he is," said Christopher, peeking around Barrel who was stooped over, looking through the bushes. "I am scared of those damn cotton mouths," he added. "He is a cotton mouth ain't he?"

They moved a little closer up the bank.

"Quiet," said Barrel, holding two fingers to his lips.

There was suddenly a flop in the water. A lower limb bounced in the still air, and the surface rippled beneath as a dark form slithered in the reflection of the stooping willow.

"There he is. There," said Christopher pointing.

"Sho nuff is."

"I wish I'd thought to bring the .22."

"We bring it next time."

"Gives me the willies."

"We'll dust his ass off when we comes back. He stays right in the bottom of that limb sunning hisself. We'll have to ease up real quiet-like."

Both stood motionless for a time, staring at the ever-widening circles of water.

"Let's check our trotline."

"Okay," Christopher said following Barrel through thick vegetation to the water's edge. "But be careful, Scratch has lots of buddies in here."

Barrel squatted and felt in the scum. A half-submerged jug floated nearby, its neck discolored by a film of moss. Finally, Barrel fished up a line tied to a rock.

"I gots it," he said, lifting it out of the water.

"Give it a tug."

The old jug bobbed with a quick jerk, then stopped, and jerked again.

"There's something on it."

"Heavy?"

"You bet. Uh huh, yeah, good and heavy sho is, real heavy."

Barrel pulled in the line slowly with both hands, one over the other, as the jug trailed bobbing along.

"Lookee here," he pulled again as a fish thrashed the water.

"Catfish?" guessed Christopher aloud.

"Uh huh, big-un, too."

The water broke again. Barrel lifted the grey catfish, letting it twist in the sun. One treble hook held through its lower lip, so Barrel held it chest-high by both ends, the fish sagging in the middle. Several other hooks hung empty on either side of the panting fish, their bait gone.

"Boy, that's a good un; I bet it's bout eight pounds," Barrel said after a thorough inspection. "Maybe ten."

Christopher reached over and felt of the mouth. "He's nice, Barrel, real nice."

"Look out, Mister Chris, he'll take off a finger real quick. They just love white meat," laughed Barrel.

Christopher removed his hand cautiously. "We're lucky the turtles didn't take care of him for us. There some big uns in here."

"That's why you gots to check it every day, real religious like," said Barrel as he sat down and worked the fish off the hook expertly.

"This ole pond is full of fish, ain't it Barrel?"

"Especially catfish, lots and lots of catfish," he said, hitting the fish in the head with a rock until it bled through the gills and lay still. "Yeah, there's plenty for alla us in the pond. Them ole turtles done sick of catfish, there's so many in here. Yes sir, nuff for everybody," he added, putting the fish on a stringer he produced from his pocket. "Sho is."

"I'll get the jug," said Christopher anxious to do something. He picked up the float and threw it back out into the pond with a splash.

"Tomorrow when we comes back to shoot ole Scratch, we'll bait her up again."

"How many we got now?"

"Almos nuff for a fry, this being so big. We'll deep fry em with onions and hushpuppies; yo hands'll be greasy for a week."

"Wonder why those turtles ain't cleaned out this pond?"

"Shoot, Mister Chris, they'll always be fish in *this* water, if'n we jus leave it alone an not fish it too hard. Lots of varmits fishing in here too – coons, snakes, turtles, them big ole cranes, too, but they don't botha nothin sides, I like to see em, think they're pretty, sho is. Don't you worry non bout it. The Lord done got it worked out, if'n we don't mess it up. We got to keep quiet about it, Chris, cause if'n we don't, we gonna have all kinds of help in here cleaning out the catfish. Folks mostly think this ole pond is dead. I ain't gonna tell nobody. This here is ours. Fact is, Mister Chris, me and you is rich."

"Why you figure we are rich, Barrel?"

"Cause we gots fish, and woods full of game, an we got time to hunt em and fish em, an there ain't nobody to bother us. If'n a man got a good gun an some shells an a fishing pole, he don't need nothin else, less it be a good dog, maybe a boat an motor. That's all he need. The secret's not learning what you needs in life, but what you can do without."

Barrel dipped the fish in the water, washing off the grass.

"Folks don't need half of the things they thinks they needs. If'n it takes a lot of money to get sumpin, chances are you don't needs it. Cept a piece of ground, a man ought to have a little piece of ground for hisself. Like that little dab o' land I gots. Not a whole lot, not too much, that'll just make em unhappy, jus enough to make an honest livin on, that's all. Make a livin so he can do right by his kids, an have time to hunt an fish. An don't be worried none bout no crazy ideas, jes leave it to the Lord. Man ought to jes live simple like."

"We rich as hell then, Barrel."

"You bet we rich, real rich, Mister Chris."

28

NGUYEN'S SQUAD ESCAPED UNDER the protection of the B-40 rockets. One man had been killed and three wounded. They were left in an aid station hidden in a tunnel. There, too, Corporal Tien had received his orders from his platoon commander to proceed down the valley and reinforce the rest of the unit now engaging an enemy village and outpost. The offensive would continue, he was told, despite the daylight conditions and the heavy pressure from American air and artillery fire. The monsoon weather would be some help, and, it was explained, the enemy fire bases were under pressure. Nguyen was not so sure, but he said nothing. He had no choice.

The grass was tall and the walking difficult, but Nguyen did not mind because it hid them from observation as they worked their way down the valley. Uncle Nhang had lectured him about camouflage, and Nguyen was very scrupulous in this regard. His men's faces were black with mud and their helmets covered with grass. Nguyen carried an RPG over his shoulder as well as an AK-47 cradled in his arm. A few days before, he had stolen binoculars from the body of an ARVN Captain, and they felt good against his hip. He liked American equipment.

But the AK-47 is better than the M-16, more reliable and more rugged, he thought. *It's better for war if things are made simple. The Americans rely too much on gadgets. There is no easy way in war, no substitute for sacrifice.* He picked up the pace.

A Marine Bronco circled overhead. Quickly Nguyen signaled his squad to freeze in the bush. After a time it flew away and began to fire at something they could not see. They rose and began walking again through the head-high grass.

It's good the Americans don't have a General Giap. Uncle Nhang says he's a genius. It was good the French didn't either. General Giap is very clever. Nguyen felt glad to be on the move again and away from the ditch in front of Fox Company. It was always better to be on the move.

Firing was heard in the distance, but it was small arms, and no one paid

130

any attention.

Nguyen had asked the Battalion political officer why it was necessary to fight anymore since the French had left the North. He had said that the South had to be liberated from imperialism before there could ever be peace and that Laos and Cambodia had to be liberated too; it was their duty to do so.

Nguyen really did not understand completely, but he had remained silent. Today he was intent on getting down the valley and continuing the attack as had been ordered. The struggle for Fox Company abated with the coming of the light; the Coke can had ruined everything so it had been cancelled except for mortar fire and other harrassment. Hopefully, the Marines there would be tied down. Nguyen was not unhappy that he had been ordered to leave. The artillery fire was getting too unbearable to do anything but lie in holes and tunnels like vermin. The new man had been killed, and Nguyen felt that it was his fault for not teaching more when he had time; the private had been very foolish and had died stupidly and unnecessarily.

But the dead man had brought news that the Americans were still bombing near Hanoi and that they had stopped for a while in other parts of the country, then started up again. Nguyen did not understand why the bombing would stop and start, or why the Americans would bomb some things and not others; it made no sense. It also made no sense why the Americans would not go into Cambodia and Laos where their bases were, but then it made no sense either why he should fight for a Southern village that was not even near his own.

The night before the attack the men had been talking about home, their families, and villages, but Nguyen made them quit, telling them that they should not do that because it only made things worse and besides, was bad luck. It did not help. The men replied that it was terrible to die so far from the graves of their fathers.

"You are not going to die tomorrow if you do not think that you are," Nguyen had said, trying to think of the correct thing to say. But one had died already, more from inexperience than bad luck. "Nguyen, we can get revenge today," he said out loud, patting the RPG gingerly with his hand. The village was very close.

29

CHRISTOPHER'S COLUMN RUMBLED DOWN the cracked asphalt toward Nam O village. They passed the perimeter wire of Fox Company. It was a brown knoll of mud, crowned with strands of interlocking concertina wire that wound round the hill like the silver web of a giant spider. Inside were sandbagged bunkers connected by rows of meandering trenches. A twin-engine helicopter squatted on the small LZ to load wounded that were hurriedly ferried up the rear ramp.

"Have the gooks didi'd, Lieutenant?" asked Burgey.

"Split for the valley, looks like."

"Any lying in the wire?"

"Must of cleaned em off, or the gooks drug them away with first light, because I can't see any," Christopher said as he swept the hill quickly with his binoculars.

"Really can't tell though," he added.

"Must'a zapped a bunch the way they was shootin; must a been boo-coo gooks last night," said Burgey as he tried to see out of the gun sight from his position below Christopher's feet.

"Horrible Hog Company will be kicking off their sweep real soon, huh, Lieutenant?"

"Yeah, real soon, we've got to hurry."

The pavement ended abruptly at the ARVN's front gate, announcing a long stretch of muddy road leading to the village. Christopher stood erect in the commander's hatch and surveyed the mountain range to the west that marked the end of the Ho Chi Minh trail. The road was by open rice paddies on either side, and his thoughts were about ambushes. Then he swung to the right and looked across more paddy water. Here, a tree line was set beneath brown hills. Over there was the South China Sea.

Christopher pulled on his goggles as the mud began to churn upwards. Feeling the tug of the shoulder holster containing his pistol, he was glad to be on the move again and away from the confines of the Battalion rear. He hated the rear and was always pleased to be back in the field.

The ARVN wire slipped quickly past as they approached a watchtower that stood on stilt-like poles. The small house on top resembled a crow's nest. In it Christopher saw his friend, the Army advisor, who, usually neat, looked disheveled and exhausted. The Captain raised a weary hand and signaled at the lead tank. Christopher returned the gesture with a wave of his arm.

The Captain cupped his hands, leaned out and yelled something that Christopher could not hear as the engine swallowed the sound like a smothered voice in a storm.

Tripper Man slowed for a disabled ARVN Jeep abandoned in the middle of the road. Its right rear tire was flat and it was riddled with bullets. A new M-16 rifle was lying in the mud, and a radio was sitting in the back seat.

"New Jeep, fucking ARVN just left," Tripper Man complained as he braked and put the tank in low gear to swing around.

"Gooks gets all the new gear; we can't get none," he added in disgust as he shifted to high gear again, quickly leaving the Jeep behind.

Coming around, Christopher saw a Buddhist Monk walking along the road towards the column. He wore a faded orange and white robe that hung the length of his body. He appeared tall for a Vietnamese, and his head was shaved.

To the right, on a slight hill above the rice paddy, was a small Buddhist temple. At its foot were four newly dug graves where the Marines had buried four NVA.

"Buddha Hill on the right," Christopher said over the intercom to the crew. "Nam O not too far, couple of more miles."

The monk did not acknowledge the column but stared ahead, walking with a steady gait like a man hypnotized. "Eat time," thought Christopher. "No sweat." They roared by him, yet he did not deviate from his course as the tank's tread churned within inches of his right shoulder.

"Crazy bastard," Tripper Man said, "all those fuckers are nuts."

The column made a turn and rolled down another road, advancing toward the village.

"Traverse right," commanded Christopher to Burgey who gripped the control handles, placed his eyes against the periscope and brought the steel turret and cannon slowly rotating to the right.

"Alpha 32, traverse left, over," commanded Christopher to Sergeant Love over the radio.

Alpha 32, which had taken up the rear position, now traversed to the left.

"Alpha 32 traversed left, over," came the quick reply.

"Affirmative, 32," responded Christopher, sliding behind the cupola of the tank commander's position. He rested against the hatch which was half-cocked to protect his back.

Though their hatches remained open, the driver and loader disappeared into the entrails of the machine, leaving Christopher exposed, peering out.

"Ninety - switch is off?" asked Christopher.

"Ninety - switch is off," replied Burgey, checking the gun switch above his head.

"Load HE," said Christopher to Harris who, standing to the left of the cannon's breach turned, steadying himself against the armour plating with his hips and shoulders, reached into the forward rack of standing shells and with both hands gently lifted the shiny brass round, and, in one fluid motion, shoved it home. With a quick snap and bounce the breach swallowed it up.

"A 32, load HE, over," repeated Christopher to Sergeant Love.

"Affirmative, 32, HE loaded, out."

"Wide open, driver."

"Yes, sir," said Tripper Man as the tank accelerated.

Like a shepherding destroyer, Christopher's tank led his flock across the open sea of paddies.

"The road been swept Lieutenant?" asked Harris sitting back down on the loader's seat.

"Yesterday; hope the ARVN and Nam O have kept them off with fire and illum."

"Maybe the gooks been too busy up in the valley," Harris crackled over the intercom.

"Yeah, trust to luck," said Christopher looking steadily at the tree line where an ambush might be hidden.

"Yes, suh, I reckon that's what we'll be doing all day, jest trusting to luck," Harris crackled back, nervously checking the stacked 90mm ammunition.

Diesel engines roaring, the tank rocked, swaying on its heavy suspension system, bouncing Christopher back and forth against the cupola. He estimated the range to the tree line at a thousand meters, so he slipped down to the seat behind the gunner and set the range-finder. This information was automatically transferred to the computer which sent it to the cannon.

"Gunner, is HE indexed in the computer?" he asked over the intercom, remembering that he should have checked the index first.

Burgey took his eyes from the periscope and looked at the white box. The ballistics index read HE. "Yes, sir, HE indexed," he replied over the intercom.

Christopher knew if they survived a mine they would be left to fight for themselves. The React had priority, and casualties were expected.

He had often bragged about the power of a tank platoon. Five tanks have almost as many cannons as an artillery battery; as many radios as a communications platoon; as many machine guns as a weapons platoon; and as many men as an infantry platoon. He had bragged he had more mobility and shock power than any unit of comparable size in the Marine Corps.

But this was not Germany, or Africa, or any romantic and glorious lightning thrusts in the desert. No J.E.B. Stuart dashes behind Yankee lines. This was Vietnam, and somehow all that fire power had gotten spread out and scattered, dissipated in the frustation of fighting a shadow enemy that did not have to win but merely avoid losing. Avoid losing, that was it; the Viet Cong simply avoided losing; and pretty soon the Americans would tire and leave as strangely as they had come.

"Trust to luck," Harris repeated like a chant over the intercom.

Christopher felt ill as he surveyed the tree line. How far? How many more yards without the blue and red flash exploding under the track.

"Machine gun switch on, " Christopher said to Burgey who flipped the firing switch to the "on" position.

"Machine gun switch is on, sir," came the reply.

Christopher ducked his head and looked over the gunner's shoulder. The machine gun was on, and the cannon's switch was off. Satisfied, he sat up again. The sky was overcast with patches of sun. The illness seemed to have subsided.

Out of the sky, an airplane appeared, first as a long dot, then gradually focusing into a twin propeller Marine Bronco that began to circle in a lazy way. It made a few passes over the mountain, then dipped one wing and swung into a steep dive towards the earth. Smoke trailed quickly, first off one wing, then the other.

"Willy Peter," thought Christopher as white phosphorous rockets sped downward, exploding on the hillside in silent billowing puffs. "Target marking," he concluded.

The plane pulled up in a slow, steep turn as orange flashes sparked from the mountainside. It gained altitude and flew toward the South China Sea, becoming a black dot again.

Then, he saw two silver objects slip from their nest above the clouds. Like swooping hawks, they plummeted. Above the diesels, he heard the phantoms pounce. Pulling upward, they sank their claws of burning orange and red napalm into the hillside. Lifting, they circled to the south over the burning gasoline, dipping their wings at an angle. Turning completely, once more they came, stooping, then lifting behind the flash and bump of bombs. The shock waves touched Christopher's face as they circled, lingered, then disappeared.

War is a disaster, he thought, watching the jets fade.

Settled among the trees, he saw the edge of the village. It was not far.

"Flashes right!" someone yelled. An automatic burped in quick flashes across the paddy from about two hundred yards.

Christopher pulled the bolt and fired the machine gun. It bounced wildly as bullets hit everywhere. He fired another inaccurate burst at the same time others began shooting. The streams of tracers careened madly about the tree line, throwing mud in the air and splattering the water with spinning fragments of earth.

The tree line fell silent.

"Charlie's shooting as badly as we are," said Christopher, clearing the fifty. "Just raise up, shoot a couple of quick bursts and duck into your hole before the shit starts flying around."

"Do any good, Lieutenant?" asked Burgey. "I couldn't tell."

"No, probably should have used the thirty."

"I never saw 'em," said Burgey still looking through the periscope which stuck out of the turret like a large wart.

"Keep eyeballing the tree line. We're not far from the village; almost in."

30

NGUYEN SET HIS PEOPLE IN very carefully. Another unit had just left; now it was simply a matter of using their holes and improving the camouflage. The village was quiet, so it was necessary for them to be even quieter. "It is better to be here than in the valley," he decided. In the valley there had been too many airplanes and too much artillery. Nguyen was at home in this little patch of jungle across from the village, and he could tell that his men were as well.

After giving instructions for the placement of the mortar, Nguyen went from position to position checking and encouraging his men. Then he returned to his hole near the end of the muddy road, pulled around more camouflage and settled in. Here he could see across the paddy to the village; all of his men had good fields of fire to the front. Scouts had been dropped for security, and now the only thing to do was hope that nothing happened at all, that they could spend a quiet day lying in the earth. Better still, they would be pulled back to the mountains. Then they could smoke and cook rice. The hunger had passed to the stage of numbness, but it was still hard not to think of food when one was not so busy. Home was an impermissible thought, and Nguyen suppressed its painful attempt to intrude into his conciousness. Instead, he busied himself with the RPG, then began sweeping the village with his binoculars.

Focusing, he swept the village defenses. There were the usual sandbagged bunkers, barbed wire decorated with red and white coke cans, claymore mines looking like little green frogs, abandoned towers, and hooches. But they did not have to make an attack. Their job was to sit tight and guard the road. "Interdiction," the Lieutenant had said to Nguyen when they spoke in the cave.

"With luck no one will come. The Marines seemed busy up the valley, and it is possible that nothing will happen here," Nguyen told himself.

A private crawled over and slithered into Nguyen's hole.

"Here's the mine," he said in a whisper, handing Nguyen the little box with black wire running out of the end toward the road.

"Good," said Nguyen, taking it in his hand, checking it then laying it on the edge of the hole near the RPG.

"You said to lengthen it and I did. You have plenty to use from this hole. It was way too short. Before, you would have to lie in the grass very near the water. This is better," added the Private, wanting Nguyen to appreciate his work.

"Yes, very good," said Nguyen. "Very good," he repeated.

"Do you think the Americans will come today?" asked the Private.

"It's possible. We are hitting the hill down the road. It's where they have that outpost we came by last night; they might send someone to help them. I hope not." Gunfire could be heard in that direction.

"Yes, last night was very hard Corporal Tien; we need to rest. The men are very tired."

"I know that."

"The attack did not go well, am I right?"

"It could have been better," said Nguyen, pretending to adjust the binoculars.

"Yes, but the Marines are hurting too, huh?"

"Of course," said Nguyen not wanting to talk anymore.

"Everyone is very sorry about the new man. He did not last long, huh, Corporal Tien?"

"Go back to your hole and try to get some rest. Maybe we'll be lucky today."

"Yes, it's our turn for some luck," said the Private before slithering away through the grass.

There was more gun fire at the hill down the road. Then things were quiet for a time. Someone crawled away to urinate, then crawled back. Nguyen looked at the village again. There was still no one in the towers; they were obviously afraid of snipers.

"Cowering in their bunkers," he decided. "We must have hurt them last night."

The sun was up fully, and, despite the wetness, Nguyen began to feel sleepy in the warmth of the early day. He closed his eyes. It would not hurt to sleep. "Things are very secure — no artillery, no planes, nothing but a terrified village that isn't even sure we're here," he concluded as he dropped off into a deep slumber.

There was fighting behind again, but Nguyen did not awake. There was firing across the village on the other end of the road, but Nguyen did not awake. A small bird flew in, then flew quickly away, but Nguyen did not see him.

Then the Private dropped into the hole shaking Nguyen.

"What is it? What's going on?" he asked, shaking his head.

"Noise!" said the Private.

"Noise?"

"Yes, noise, listen!"

Nguyen sat up, cupping his hands to his ears.

"Tanks!" he said between gritted teeth.
"Tanks?"
"Yes! Tanks."
"Where?"
"Coming to us!"

31

THE VILLAGE APPEARED DESERTED as Christopher led the convoy past the perimeter of barbed wire into its center.

Here was a clump of hooches crowded within a thick grove of trees. A mangy pariah of a dog trotted away; a withered Mama San scooped up a naked child and disappeared into a hole.

Then an American stuck his head out of a grass hooch. Christopher dismounted.

"Where the hell you been?" he yelled as he stepped out and walked toward them.

Nam O was an island surrounded by rice paddies; it was isolated by watchtowers on either end, tightly encircled barbed wire, and mines. Lately it had become part of the pacification program, which in the words of Major Craig, "was to separate the fishes from the sea." Craig had read Mao.

Christopher watched the hollow-eyed sergeant saunter up as Lieutenant Malone got out of his truck and jogged over.

"Sergeant Garcia, here. NCO in charge of this here little ville," he said. Sergeant Garcia was medium height with straight black hair that hung limply over his tired face. He carried no weapon, was hatless, and he had long since taken off his flak jacket. The only way Christopher could tell his rank was from ink scribble above his left breast pocket: "Sgt. Garcia,A+."

"What's up Lieutenant?" he asked.

"Relief column to Falcon," answered Malone.

"You're a relief here, too, I'll tell you that," replied Garcia, putting his hands in his pockets and smiling a slight, painful smile.

"What's going on?"

"I got one KIA and two hit pretty bad, five left, and a Doc. Been in the shit all night."

"The ARVN?"

"Split, except for three, and one of them is dead. Like I say, we've been up to our asses since the sun went down. Gooks almost bought the farm; hadn't been so interested in going up the Valley, they would have."

"Villagers?" asked Malone.

"Nothing but old Mama Sans, Papa Sans, and Baby Sans, man; the rest didi'd with the ARVN or Charlie; not much around to pacify," he forced a smile again. "Kinda hard to win their hearts and minds."

"Fuck 'em, shrugged Malone.

"That's what I say, fuck 'em. Fuck them and the rest of this goddamn country," added Garcia, the smile gone.

"Can your wounded hang on?"

"No telling. Watermelon is really hit bad; Waterman, but we call him Watermelon; the rest'll make it, Doc says, if we can get em outa here real soon-like, like real quick. Watermelon is all fucked up though."

"We'll lift them out of Falcon once we get this area half-way secure," said Malone.

"Falcon's really been into it, too. We had good contact with 'em until our radio went down. ARVN skyed out with the rest of them. We've been deaf, dumb and scared since midnight."

"Everybody's been into it, really swarming all over the area," Malone put in. "Big offensive everywhere."

"Sure looked that way. Flares in the air all goddamn night, helicopters all over – gooks must be trying to prove something, acting like they're kinda irritated with us a little."

"What's the skinny, Garcia?" yelled a Navy corpsman inside a hut.

"Tell 'em to hold on, Doc; they're going out on a chopper from Falcon. Just tell 'em to hang on."

"Garcia, we're setting up our headquarters here. You got any weapons left?" asked Malone.

"Two M-60 machine guns and a mortar left by the ARVN."

"Okay, with our mortars and machine guns, we'll set up a base of fire here in order to cross that rice paddy. Any activity over there recently?"

"Not recently. Turned quiet all of a sudden, but Charlie's around, you can count on that. I imagine things'll start happening if you try to cross that paddy."

"I'll leave a fireteam here with the mortars. Your wounded will come out by truck once we relieve Falcon. They got a couple of Engineers at Falcon, right?"

"Right. Supposed to have, if they ain't been zapped."

"As soon as things are secure, we'll sweep the road and bring up any casualties. Might have to bring them up by tank, I don't know, but you can't go back the way we came; you'll just get ambushed on the road. We ran into some gooks on the way in."

"The sooner the better."

"Okay, casualties out Falcon. Meantime, help out with the people you got left to lay down some fire so we can cross that rice paddy. It's the only way, right?"

"Yes, sir. No other. That's if you want to go to Falcon."

Lieutenant Malone gathered Christopher and his NCO's into a huddle while Sergeant Garcia went to set up his weapons. Malone spread out his laminated plastic map on the ground.

"One more time, real quick. First, Arty mission by Delta Battery, then base of fire with mortars, tanks and machine guns; lift on command. Fireteam from first squad stay behind. First and second squads across to the left of the road, third squad to the right. Before we jump off, everything stops but mortars, which continue until I fire a red flare, alternate signal by radio. When we get to that first paddy dike in the middle, tanks assault out of the ville, down and across the road into the tree line. Do not fire until you get past us, Chris. When the tanks go through the middle, down the road, I'll fire the red flare, mortars lift, and it's over the top and into the trees. Remember, assault through the objective, not just to it. We'll lay down a base of fire before the tanks reach even with us. Mortars fire smoke first and last to obscure things in the tree line. If there's anybody there, I want them to be blinded by smoke, okay?"

"No sweat on the mission, Lieutenant," spoke up the Artillery F.O. from Delta Battery. "It's cleared."

"Machine guns?" spoke up a Corporal.

"Right, two that belong here stay here. Deliver overhead fire *if requested*, but only if requested. I won't ask for it unless we get pinned down in the paddy. The other two go with us to deliver fire into the trees once we reach that paddy dike and before the dash into the woods, okay? Questions?"

There was silence.

"My watch says 0713. We'll kick off support fire at 0730," he said, glancing around as everybody set their watches to 0713. "Once over, we regroup and everybody on line for the sweep to Falcon. We'll worry about the blocking force later."

The group dissolved. Christopher started back to his tanks now positioned by Sergeant Love at the eastern edge of the village. He paused briefly, stared through the foliage at the tree line and lighted a cigarette.

32

CHRISTOPHER'S CIGARETTE HAD ALMOST burned to the end as the cream of the Arkansas Delta crowded through the Shaw's front door. It was the holiday season and they were giving their annual party. The house was filled with people. Past the hallway to the right was a large hors d'oeuvre table where a doctor crowded near a banker for the cheese dip and their wives struggled bravely to manage the jumbo shrimp Queeny had impaled on toothpicks. In the living room to the left an elderly black man in a tuxedo played swing music from the forties on a Steinway, and Barrel, in a white waist jacket and black satin pants, circulated among the guests with whiskey refills perched on a silver tray.

Conrad and Elizabeth stood dutifully near the door.

"So good to see you," said Wilbur Webb, handing a servant his coat. "Miss Margaret couldn't come, she sends her regards," he added.

"I'm so sorry; is she ill?" asked Elizabeth, pretending concern.

"Yes, I'm afraid it's the flu."

"How about a drink?" asked Conrad, concluding Webb needed one.

"Bourbon and water."

Barrel came with the drinks.

"Here you is, Mister Wilbur," said Barrel.

"Thank you so much, Barrel, how have you been?" said Webb, taking the drink and wrapping it tightly in a little fat fist.

"I'm fine, thank you, suh. How's the lawyering coming?"

"Very well, thank you; they keep me busy, Barrel."

"Oh yes, suh, I knows you be busy all right."

"You been working hard?"

"Yes, suh, Mister Conrad, bout to work us to def this year, sho is."

"You know, Conrad, I think at least half these people here are my clients or spouses of clients," he said, turning from Barrel and sipping his drink.

"You've obviously built up a very successful practice."

"Well, thank you, but I go to so many of these types of parties out of a sense of obligation, you know; but yours and Elizabeth's are always special and real fun, just a delight. And you have such a lovely home. Miss Margaret was so disappointed."

"Well, thank you, Wilbur; we are sorry she's not feeling well. Please excuse me, but I must check on dinner with the cook. She's new and it worries me to leave her alone for such a long time. God knows what she's done to the duck. Will y'all forgive me?" Elizabeth said, not waiting for an answer and walking to the kitchen.

"Surely," said Wilbur, sipping again.

"Yours is mostly office work, isn't it, Wilbur, I mean you never get to court much do you anymore?"

"Some, not much. Mostly business clients. It's cleaner, more orderly practice than that trial stuff. Not as messy."

"Still do the bank's business?"

"Of course; and it's a good account," he said, munching peanuts taken from a nearby bonbon tray.

"I see."

"Very good, indeed. I try to keep them happy."

"A bloodsucker, a real bloodsucker," Conrad remembered Christopher saying one night by the campfire with the hounds out of hearing in the Bayou Blanc bottoms. "Yes, but he's good, Son," Conrad had said. He recalled this with some vague discomfort now as he watched Webb gobble the nuts off the heel of his palm, spilling several carelessly on the rug.

Conrad felt vaguely guilty about his relationship with Webb. He had not always been so friendly. It was only after Conrad had risen from the status of a poor man's son to that of successful farmer that Webb's attitude had warmed in his direction. In fact, it was just after his first good year that Webb asked him to join his church. Conrad had politely declined, preferring instead to continue going to his mother's little country church. Elizabeth preferred it there, too, and he had no desire for fancy "city" churches in Frenchman's Bluff. Conrad was still considered "new rich" in Wattensaw County; he suspected that this was still his lawyer's secret opinion. But Conrad had always felt himself to be a man of the people, and it was this feeling that had forced him to give up his flirtation with serious politics. He was realistic enough to know that. Indeed, a young liberal governor had dragged them both down to defeat for a third term when Conrad had fallen under his irresistible spell in the early fifties. No, that was finished, and he needed Webb to do business. His family and land had to come first, but he did not like him and never would. And it was obvious that shortly Webb would need another drink.

"Where's your oldest boy?"

"Gilbert? Army. Overseas," Webb swelled again.

"What doing?"

"Two years."

"No, I mean what field?"

"Judge advocate," said Webb, chasing the salt off his lips with a shot of bourbon, several peanuts clearly visible on the rug.

"Really? Where?"

"Germany."

"I see. Then to Vietnam?"

"No. He made sure he had a contract for Germany, part of the deal."

"I see. I know you are relieved."

"Well, we were quite pleased," he said, shifting his weight, stepping on the nuts and grinding them into the carpet.

"Sure, I can understand, I guess. He's doing his bit."

"We're proud and relieved," he said, gulping the last of the drink and eating his ice.

"At least he's not shirking his duty."

"Right. I have no truck with those who run off to Canada; they're cowards and traitors, all of them, as far as I am concerned."

"Not like going to Germany."

"Not at all," agreed Webb as he reached for another handful of nuts, which he mixed with the chopped ice.

"Can I get you another drink?" Conrad asked.

"Please, just a splash."

"Barrel," said Conrad, reaching for the glass and catching Barrel's eye behind the bar.

The pianist switched smoothly to another song as Barrel walked over to get the empty glass.

"Bourbon and water, suh?" he asked taking the glass.

"Yes, Barrel, don't bruise the bourbon, if you please."

"Mister Conrad?"

"No, I'm fine, thank you, Barrel."

"One bourbon and water coming up," he said ambling off to the bar looking very uncomfortable in his black bow tie and dinner jacket.

"Chris still in Vietnam?"

"Yes, but he's short."

"I'm sorry, I don't get the lingo."

"Oh, well, 'short' means that he doesn't have much time left.

"I see."

"Got a month to do or so, then home, we hope."

"Worried about him?"

"Well, we try not to. It's hard on Elizabeth."

"Of course. We worry so about Gilbert, you know how those crazy German drivers are on the Autobahn, dangerous as hell."

"Sure."

"We'll be glad to get him home. I need some help in the office. Oh, he's having a lark, but we wish he were home."

"I understand."

"I know you'll be glad to get Chris home."

"Of course, very much."

"Where is he?"

"Somewhere outside of Da Nang; he moves around a lot."

"What's he gonna do when he gets out, has he decided?"

"I'm not sure, he talks about coming home and farming, but I am not sure if he will be happy doing that. He loves the out of doors, but I don't know if he wants to farm."

"Let 'em have some rein for awhile. He may go back to school, raise a little hell, then he'll come around."

"How about your boy? Gilbert coming home to practice with you, you say?"

"Sees it as a grand opportunity."

"I know you're looking forward to it."

The door bell rang.

"Excuse me," said Conrad going to the door.

"Surely."

The door opened to Nanna Sue and W.R. Hotchely, Jr. who owned a Frenchman's Bluff tractor dealership.

"Dear, I'm so glad to see y'all," said Elizabeth, crossing the room quickly.

"This is Wilbur Webb, Nanna Sue."

"I know Miss Nanna Sue," replied Webb unctiously.

"Why yes, we've met several times," Nanna Sue cooed, her husband handing the coats to Conrad.

"Business good, W.R.?" said Webb.

"Trying to stay ahead of you and Delta State."

"Why, hasn't the bank always given you good service, W.R.?"

"I ain't complaining."

"Have you tried their new Delta Dollars plan for all that money you been making? It's a good way to invest."

"How about a drink?" asked Conrad, handing the coats to the waiting servant.

"Please, Senator."

"Everybody's in high cotton tonight; your house is so beautiful," said Nanna Sue.

"Can I get you anything?" asked Conrad.

"White wine, if you have it."

"Sure."

Conrad looked at Barrel again who seemed occupied behind the bar talking to the bartender, hired for the evening. Webb, who had finished his ice, cast an anxious glance in the same direction.

"Barrel, white wine for Mrs. Hotchely, please," said Conrad across the room.

"Nanna Sue has invited me to go shopping with her in Memphis sometime. Isn't that nice of her? That's her hometown, and she does know her way round so good."

"Sounds like fun," said Conrad, pretending interest.

Barrel brought the drinks to the Hotchelys.

"You forgot me," muttered Webb.

"Oh, yes suh, I'm sorry, coming right up, Mister Wilbur," said Barrel, going back to the bar.

"I am so glad to be here, Conrad," added Nanna Sue nibbling from a cracker covered in yellow cheese.

"Thank you. I'm glad you were able to come," said Conrad.

"I do love your cute piano player; where did y'all get him from?"

"Where did you find him, Elizabeth?" Conrad said.

"Oh, he plays all over – Little Rock, Memphis, Pine Bluff. I don't really know where he's from; a friend found him for me. Isn't he good?"

"Sure is. I think I'll use him myself sometime. It's hard to find one that knows anything but nigra music."

"Oh, he knows everything," Elizabeth added.

"This is such a delightful crowd. I've heard that y'all's parties are always so good," said Nanna Sue, surveying the crowd.

"Thank you, dear, it's so good of you to come," said Elizabeth trying not to sound bored as the two turned away, leaving the men.

"Oh, we're so happy to be here," cooed Nanna Sue in return. "I do love Wilbur Webb so much – he's so nice and friendly to me, always just a doll. So kind and such a gentleman. Don't you think so, dear?"

"Oh, yes. . ."

"And Conrad. . .Well, we're just so proud of him, he's just marvelous. . .it's just great the way he has carved his way in the world isn't it? After all he's been through, you know, hard times, the war and all. . .everyone admires him so much, they really do, dear; you're a lucky girl. Do you know that? And you're so cute together, a darling couple – everyone says so. . ."

"Come on dear, I want you to meet some other people. We'll leave the men to talk business," she said taking Nanna Sue by her elbow and leading her away.

"Oh, grand," she said, trying not to spill her wine.

"Junior Hotchely's wife, she's sumpin' else," Webb grunted indignantly as he glanced in the direction of Barrel, now fumbling around for a clean cocktail glass.

"They haven't been married long, have they Wilbur?"

"Naw, bout a year. She's a big social climber. Bout to pee on herself that y'all invited her and Junior."

"I do a lot of business with him. He's a helluva good turkey hunter, too. We belong to the same hunting club."

"Oh yeah, he's a fine fella, real fine fella."

"You don't hunt do you, Wilbur?"

"No, never did care anything about it, Conrad. Can't stand to kill anything."

"Your dad never took you when you were a boy?"

"Too busy building up his law practice."

"I see. Your dad did the bank's work in the early days, too?"

"Oh, yes. They've always used us. Delta State has been good to us over the years."

Conrad remembered the foreclosures.

"I see old man Root is here."

"Yes, he and his wife came early."

"Only one in town. Maybe someday he'll get some competition."

"I'd rather farm."

"You had a good year?"

"Good year. Wish Christopher were home."

"Conrad, tell Barrel we'll be needing to round everybody up soon toward the dining room," Elizabeth said, standing by two physicians near the living room fireplace.

"The only real cases of diffuse intravascular coagulation that I have seen recently have been associated with trauma and, of course, irreversible shock," said one doctor, poking the fire with a brass poker.

Barrel put several drinks on a tray and returned to Webb and Conrad.

"Thank you, Barrel," said Webb with obvious relief.

"Yes, suh."

"Miss Elizabeth says we'll have to be heading em in the direction of the dining table, Barrel, real soon like," Conrad said.

"Yes, suh, it better be soon, else'n these peoples be falling all over day selves the way they drinking fo dinner."

"Maybe you better shorten up on the booze."

"If'n I do that they be hollering bout bruising the whiskey," said Barrel looking at Webb. "That drink all right, Mr. Wilbur?"

"Fine, thank you, Barrel."

"Anyway, we'll have to start heading them in pretty soon."

"Yes, suh."

"Saunter over and check on Miss Elizabeth's drink, and see if she needs you to do anything for her. You know how she worries at these things."

"Yes, suh. I don't know why she worry so much, an if'n she do, why she have it in the firs place? But I checks on her."

Barrel strolled over to Elizabeth who was stranded with the two doctors.

"I'm so glad you came over, Barrel. We need to start everybody in so you might slow down on the whiskey," she said lifting a glass of wine delicately.

"Yessum."

"Thank you," said one of the men to Barrel who was standing by with a tray of drinks. "You are a fine fella," he said, replacing an empty.

"Yes, suh. Thought you might be needing me."

"And you, Doctor, how bout my las drink here. Miss Elizabeth done tole me to slow down so you better take it while you gots the chance."

"Thanks for the warning, Barrel," said the other one reaching for the last cocktail. "Good fixin's, I can tell," he said wiggling the diamond ring on his little finger against the glass of bourbon.

"How you been, Barrel?" asked one.

"Fine, thanks, an you, suh?"

"Busy. When's Chris coming home?"

"Soon," answered Elizabeth.

"We sho be glad, too. Seem like he been gone forever cross the pond. Can't hunt or fish with nobody but myself; Mister Conrad don't care nothin about it much no mo with Mister Chris gone, and to tell you the truth, I don't like it as much neither with him not here," said Barrel. "Be glad to get him home, das fo sho, uh huh."

"I know y'all will," added the doctor drinking half the drink.

"I guess I better start shooin folks away from the trough."Barrel said to himself walking away.

"You want some mo nut, Mister Wilbur?" asked Barrel as he passed by and looked at the empty bonbon tray.

"No, thank you, I'll wait for dinner."

"Yes, suh."

"You know, Barrel is a great man in his own way," Conrad remembered Christopher saying one night as they sat drinking bourbon under the stars listening to the dogs run. It was also a December, and Christopher was home from the University.

"A good soul," Conrad had replied throwing another branch on the fire, making it blaze.

"He knows that happiness doesn't come from what you have, but what you are. What you feel. Your soul."

"You're right, Christopher, he knows a lot; learned it from nature," said Conrad, putting the pint bottle back into his game pocket.

"That's why I love it here in the darkness under the moon, near a fire, swallowed by the forest," said Christopher never taking his eyes from the flames that danced on his face in ghostly patterns.

"Where are the dogs, I wonder?" asked Conrad after a pause.

"Lost in the Bayou Blanc bottoms."

33

"WHAT THE HELL IS GOING ON at Nam O?" roared Zell at Craig. "We're trying to raise them now, sir."

"Hurry the fuck up. I'm tired of being in the dark about it. They are just screwing around out there, Craig."

"Yes, sir, we're making every effort to get them now, sir," the Major answered, opening the pop-top of a Coca-Cola can.

"They're just fiddle-fucking around, that's all."

"Yes, sir."

"Stalling, that's what they're doing, stalling. And I thought you said that Malone was the best grunt Lieutenant in this Battalion."

"Right, sir, he is."

"Well, if that's the case we're in piss-poor shape, Craig, you know that, piss-poor shape."

"Yes, sir," he said sipping the Coke.

"Jesus, the Marine Corps is turning to shit, you know that, to shit."

"I think that they may be hung up trying to cross that rice paddy, Colonel."

Colonel Zell turned and stared directly at Craig with puffy eyes as he scratched a roll of fat hanging over his web belt. "What fucking rice paddy?"

"What rice paddy?"

"Yes, what fucking rice paddy, Major?"

"The rice paddy east of Nam O on the road up to Falcon, sir; the one we discussed earlier, sir."

"That rice paddy?"

"Yes, Colonel, that one," said Craig, eyeing Zell from behind the safety of the tipped Coca Cola can.

"Shit, I thought you meant a real rice paddy; that one at Nam O couldn't be much more than about a hundred yards. That's no goddamn problem, Major.

They ought to punch right across there, just punch right across. What do they want? Jesus, they got tanks, mortars, machine guns; what the hell do they want? Huh? What do they want, for us to call in the world, the whole fucking world for them? Air, artillery, B-52s, naval gunfire, nukes – is that what they want, the whole bloody world? They afraid somebody might get hurt, is that it? Shit,when I was in Korea, we stacked frozen bodies around us like logs. You ever hear the sound of machine gun bullets hitting frozen Chinamen, Major, huh? With those goddamn Chinese bugles blowing over the snow, you ever hear that? Shit, Major, this ain't a war; we just think it's a war. This is military masturbation, that's what this is, just a bloody game. Well, war ain't a goddamn game, and we better get used to that Major. The gooks ain't playing no games."

"Yes,sir."

"We thought this shit would be easy, huh, just a pushover. Well, I got news for them. This shit is going to be forced down our throats many more times, Major, a lot fucking more, you know that?"

"Yes sir."

"The gooks are tired of fucking around, and they ain't playing no more games; they're bout to get this show on the road. You know that?"

There was silence in the Bunker as Major Craig stood motionless, drinking the Coca Cola. Zell swigged down the rest of his beer, belched, and turned away like a tired bull swinging in confusion.

"I think I have them, sir," spoke up a private shyly.

"Have what?" asked Zell.

"The platoon, sir, I think I have them in the clear, sir," he explained.

"Goddamn it, Craig, talk to them," he ordered, reaching into the styrofoam ice chest for another beer.

"Bushmaster, this is Red Dancer. Give me a sitrep, over," said the Major, taking the receiver from the private's hand.

"Red Dancer, Bushmaster, go."

"Bushmaster, Red Dancer, how do you read me, over."

"Red Dancer, Bushmaster, coming in garbled, over," cracked back the voice in Nam O as machine gun fire rattle in the background of the transmission. Zell popped the beer.

"Bushmaster, give me a sitrep, over."

"Red Dancer, Bushmaster, we got gooks in the tree line, we think, over."

"They think they may be in contact, sir," said Craig.

"They THINK!" blustered Zell, "Jesus, the Marine Corps is turning to shit right before my very eyes, right before my very eyes."

"Bushmaster, let me talk to your Actual," ordered Craig, turning away from Colonel Zell.

"Red Dancer, Bushmaster, he's busy right now, sir."

"Bushmaster, this is Three, you understand. Major Craig and I want to talk to your Actual right now," he repeated nearly spilling his Coca Cola.

"Red Dancer, Bushmaster, you are coming in garbled, go," spoke the voice in a crisp response with machine gun fire again stuttering over the crackle of the radio traffic.

"Who is this shitbird?" demanded Craig, raising his voice to the radio operator.

"I don't know," he lied.

"Well, I'll have his ass if the gooks don't," replied Major Craig as he jerked the receiver, spilling the Coca Cola into the private's lap.

"Clean up that mess, damn it," he said to the private who was rubbing the wet spot on his lap.

"Bushmaster, this is Major Herman Craig, do you hear me, and I want to talk to your Actual, you understand, your CO, right now and no fucking around!"

The Major released the hand switch to listen for a response, but there was nothing but static coming in over the squawk box. All eyes in the bunker were transfixed to it like men in a submarine under attack.

Lieutenant Colonel Zell broke the silence at last. "That little shitbird is playing games, Craig."

"I know, sir."

"Try it again."

"Yes, sir."

"Bushmaster, Red Dancer, over."

"Bushmaster, Red Dancer, over," repeated Craig again after a pause.

"Red Dancer, Bushmaster, over," said the voice mechanically after a time.

"Bushmaster, this is Red Dancer. I want you to know that I am very tired of playing games, over," he said slowly as if talking to a child.

"Red Dancer, Bushmaster, you are coming in garbled, over."

"Bushmaster, Red Dancer, I hope that you realize. . ."

"Red Dancer, Bushmaster, wait one, out," the voice interrupted.

"Damn!" muttered Craig under his breath.

"Jesus, I'm going to have the whole lot strung up by their balls, Craig, if we don't get some positive movement out there damn soon," said Zell.

"Red Dancer, Bushmaster, over," cracked the voice over the radio.

"Go ahead, Bushmaster. This is Red Dancer," responded Craig quickly.

"Red Dancer, Bushmaster. The Actual says he's real busy and he will give you a sitrep when he gets some time, over."

"Give me that goddamn receiver," said Zell. "You little shitass, this is Lieutenant Colonel Zell, you understand, and I want to talk to that Lieutenant of yours right-fucking-now, you read me, son, right now!" said Zell snatching the receiver away from Craig.

"Roger, unknown station, you are coming in all garbled and broken up, over," said the voice.

"Who is this smart little bastard, Craig?"

"I don't know, sir, but I'll find out as soon as this operation is over."

"You do that, Craig, you do that, and have his young ass on my carpet as soon as possible, you understand?"

"Yes, sir."

"And that Lieutenant, too; both those damn Lieutenants as a matter of fact. I want both their asses, if the gooks don't get em."

"Yes, sir."

"The whole Marine Corps is turning to shit right before my very eyes," he repeated to the twelve-foot reinforced ceiling.

"Red Dancer, over," came the voice again.

"Yes, go ahead. This is Colonel Zell," he responded with mock courtesy.

"Red Dancer, Bushmaster, my Actual wants me to tell you that he is laying down a base of fire before moving on the objective as he planned, sir. Oh, he says Nam O is secure, he told me to report, and says too that he will give you a sitrep most rickey-tick, sir, over."

"Thank you so much," said Zell breathing heavily.

"Red Dancer, Bushmaster, over," came the voice again.

"Yes, go ahead, Bushmaster."

"Red Dancer, Bushmaster, you are welcome, out."

34

LEAVING THE CONFERENCE WITH Malone, Christopher rounded a truck coming upon two Corpsmen trying to put a man into a body bag. His feet were in but the torso would not go. The arms hung down awkwardly by his side, reminding Christopher of a rag doll sitting in a shoe box. The Corpsmen fumbled, cursing as the arms flailed about grotesquely, lurching limply this way and that. Finally, they folded them together and lowered the body into its rubber grave. One of the Corpsmen zipped the bag shut over the staring blue eyes. It was a lean, unblemished face with smooth young skin pulled tightly back over the high cheek bones. As if in protest, his blond hair stirred in the cool breeze the instant the zipper smothered him shut.

Christopher stood frozen. He had seen this before, but his reaction was always the same. A familiar nausea seized him, and he thought that he might vomit. He was ill again.

Why am I ill again? he wondered.

But he knew why he was ill. He was ill about the war in which he so desperately wanted to survive; he was ill about those who had not and wouldn't, those who did and didn't care; he was ill about those who were to come full of illusions and those who weren't. He was ill about it all, about what had happened to him, how he had gotten here like the prisoner of some malicious fate plotted even before his birth. Time and fate. The Black Prince of fate and time that seemingly set our lives immutably in stone. But worst of all, it was the terror, the violence, the utter madness that sliced through one's illusion of permanent conciousness like a vulgar joke told on the day of one's death that made him ill. It was that which made him nauseous as he waited to cross one-hundred and fifty yards of rice paddy in a steel machine.

God forbid, he said to himself. *God forbid that I should vomit like a damn coward.* He turned away and walked with head down toward his waiting tanks.

"What was his name?" he heard a Corpsman ask behind him.

"McDonnah," came the reply. "Killed last night, zapped on patrol, just when the shit hit the fan."

"Lucky there weren't more, huh?"

"Yeah, no shit. No doubt there'll be before this day is over."

"McDonnah, huh, must be Irish."

"Yeah, tag says he's Catholic, gotta be Irish."

Christopher turned after stopping again. "I want him to see a priest," he said quietly to the surprised Corpsman who had not noticed Christopher.

"Sir?"

"Get him to a priest when you get back," he repeated.

"Jesus, Lieutenant, he's dead."

"I don't give a damn. I want him to see a priest. He might want to contact his family or something. We need to do the right thing."

"Yes, sir, I'll see that it's taken care of," said the other Corpsman.

"Fine."

"I'll take care of it."

"Right," added Christopher, walking off again.

"I didn't know Lieutenant Shaw was Catholic," commented one Corpsman as Christopher walked away.

"He ain't."

"What is he?"

"Shit, nothing, I guess. Just figures it's the thing to do or something," he added, picking up one end of the body bag.

"Yeah, makes him feel better, I reckon," grunted the other as he gripped the feet and they swung the body into the back of the truck like a bale of hay. "It always makes everybody feel better."

Quentin broke his watch, thought Christopher, still nauseous.

"Lieutenant. Lieutenant Shaw," spoke up Harris.

Quentin sat looking backwards on a train at a darky on a mule, thought Christopher as the uncontrolled thought intruded into his consciousness. *Quentin sat looking backward on the train.*

"Lieutenant, sir?" asked Harris again.

"Yes, what is it?"

"Sergeant Love wants to know if we should assemble the troops."

"Yes, of course, tell him I'm coming."

"Yes, sir. You all right, Lieutenant?"

"Yes, I'm fine. I'll be right there."

"You looks pale, sir."

"I'm fine, Harris, fine. Ham-and-mothers made me sick this morning, that's all; I'm fine. I'm on my way."

"Yes, sir, I'll tell Sergeant Love."

Quentin Compson broke his watch, he thought again as the Marine left him. *Why would he do that? Why did he break his watch? Would Barrel know? Why would Barrel know? He doesn't worry his head about things like that. Would Conrad? Would Conrad know? Maybe. To destroy time and history, to not have to forever look backwards from the train. You are where you've been not where you're going; there is no future, only the past. No that can't be, the past is the future. You are what you've been; there is no future, only history unfolding itself into the future, unraveling itself, always looking backward like on the train. Like that young man in the body bag, our fate carved on the face of a rock. It's all a dream, a riddle, madness.*

Christopher shook his head slightly like a man trying to stay awake. He thought he still might get sick.

I wish I could look at a dead Marine without thinking about it. I wish I could do anything without thinking about it, anything, anything at all. "History is a nightmare from which I am trying to awake." The nausea gripped him as he struggled to control his thoughts. He felt faint.

Christopher looked at his watch as a machine gun started firing in the edge of the village. It was 0731 hours; the support fire was late. *It's time,* he thought. *I've got to go. We've got to get to Falcon; it's time to get moving.*

"Lieutenant, sir," yelled Harris as he looked around the side of the tank.

"Yes?"

"We're ready."

"Yes, Lieutenant, we're ready," said Sergeant Love, looking over Harris' shoulder.

"Coming," said Christopher, as he broke into a fast walk.

"I've filled em in already, Lieutenant," said Love.

"Good. Our mortar fire'll start in a minute. Mount up and let's pull to the edge of the ville; we'll shoot into the tree line on radio command from Malone."

"Right, sir," said Love.

The men scrambled and the engines started with a loud rumble, belching out smoke as they moved to the eastern end of the village to begin firing across the paddy.

The Artillery Forward Observer squatted casually next to Lieutanant Malone.

"What's the hot skinny, Sergeant?" asked Malone.

"Wait one, sir," he said taking another look at the distant treeline sighting with his compass.

"Let me talk," he said to his radio operator who handed him the receiver. "Got to check with the Battery," he added, now talking to Delta Battery.

"We're clear," he said after a pause.

"Let er rip; we're late now."

"Right," said the F.O. as he spoke to the Battery again. He let the radio receiver drop between his knees as he looked back at the tree line.

"Rounds out, sir."

Suddenly there was a shrill whistle and two white phosphorous rounds plopped quietly into the paddy water in front of them.

"Add one hundred, fire for effect," he said over the radio.

"Firing for effect, sir, with HE."

"Great."

"Rounds on the way; heat for Charlie."

The white smoke from the artillery rounds hung heavy in the air as the Marines crouched behind the paddy dike near the edge of the village.

Again a whistle, then a loud crack – *carump, carump, carump, carump* – detonated in the far trees as the high explosive rounds shattered the silence. The opening stage of the assault that had begun with the light signal of phosphorous smoke now shifted to the base destruction of high explosive

155

rounds. *Carump, carump, carump* cracked the high explosive rounds from Delta's 105 mm cannons again. *Carump, carump, carump* whistled and split through the trees across the paddy.

"Repeat," said the F.O. into the receiver.

Another whistle, crack, *carump, carump, carump, carump* fell staccato once more into the foliage.

"Burn em up, burn em up. The Cannon-Cockers are doing their thing," yelled Thompson lying beside Malone, squirming with excitement.

"That's all for now, Lieutenant. Won't give us no more heat for now," yelled the F.O. "That's all they can spare for us."

"Outstanding Sergeant, out-fucking-standing," said Malone.

Quickly he gave the command to the mortars who started their metallic twang and rump-rump-firing across the clearing into the objective. Machine gun tracers arched busily into the mud-and-flash explosions kicked up by the mortar shells. Christopher traversed the turret around, aimed into the sight, and ranged-out the range finder. *One hundred and fifty yards, pointblank,* he thought as he gave the order to fire.

The breach kicked back, and the tank rocked with an explosion while the cannon rounds cracked into the trees and burst green and yellow at the unseen enemy, as over and over again, the tanks poured out fire. Christopher forgot his nausea. The smoke mingled with white phosphorous and obscured the target. It all hung together in a grey and white cloud above the paddy water. The machine gun tracers looked like red summer bees swarming through an evening fog.

Surely no one could survive that, he thought, watching the smoking target through his gunsight.

"Right, right," yelled Tripper Man. "Put out some more heat, Burgey," he yelled over the intercom.

"Gooks in the hurt locker now," added Harris peeking out of the loader's hatch.

Sergeant Love's tank stopped firing its cannon and began shooting a machine gun, playing the red tracers in an undulating wave like a man calmly watering trees with a garden hose. Men lay prone in the grass and weeds, firing their M-16s, while more mortars lobbed onto the target in rapid succession, and Hot Tamale on one knee cooly lifted grenades with his "blooper."

Colored pins on a map, mused Christopher. *That's all we are, just small marks on a piece of paper. These men brought together by this queer fate will never achieve this intensity again. Hate it as they will, life will never be the same,* he thought as he raised up and pressed the butterfly on the .50 caliber machine gun.

It was 0745, and Quentin Compson's watch had vanished from Christopher's thoughts.

"Damn," cursed Lieutenant Malone, lowering his binoculars. "We're late, and the only thing those clowns can do is bug us with radio traffic."

"Yes, sir," said Stubmeyer.

"Keep stalling, that's all we can do, or they'll be trying to run this circus themselves. Just stall. I'll ride the heat later."

"I told 'em you were busy, sir," answered the Lance Corporal. "I can tell you

156

they were pissed, for sure, real pissed, sir."

"I don't give a damn. If this turns out all right, they'll pat me on the back; if not, they'll have my ass no matter how much I chitchat on the horn, right?"

"Right, sir, the proof's in the fucking pudding, sir," grinned Stubmeyer. *They were right about Malone; he's got some sense,* thought Stubmeyer as he returned to his radio in the village.

"Pass the word to cease fire," Malone added, turning to Thompson, operating the platoon's net.

"Yes, sir," said Thompson, picking up the radio and giving the order.

"Except for the mortars, I want them to continue firing as planned," he said.

Thompson nodded as the mortars kept up a slow, steady barrage into the trees. The outgoing clang and muffled explosions of the mortars continued, but the battlefield seemed oddly peaceful as silence and smoke drifted through the heavy air.

Lieutenant Malone, still standing with his little headquarters at the village edge, swept the trees once again with his glasses. There still was no sign of the North Vietnamese. "Okay," he said after inhaling deeply, "tell Corporal Westover to move out to the right of the road as planned."

"Yes, sir."

"Second and Third Squads move out to the left; I'll be with them, and tell Stubmeyer to tell Craig that we are assaulting across the paddy."

"Yes, sir," repeated Thompson as he relayed the instructions.

Malone watched the thin, green line of Marines slowly emerge from the grass into the open and walk abreast. Waiting until the line formed together, he fell in behind, with Thompson by his side at a fast walk.

Eerie, thought Christopher as quiet fell over the scene, punctuated only by the slow cadence of regulated mortar fire.

The infantry slogged through the mud and ankle-deep water in an irregular wave; yet, there was no enemy fire from the tree line, completely obscured by smoke. The sun was hidden by dark clouds. The line continued forward.

Christopher looked down at Lance Corporal Burgey, seated motionless at his feet. He was resting his forehead against the rubber covering of the gunsight like a kneeling supplicant. Harris, stationed to his left, sat limply on the loader's seat, head down, lost in thought. Tripper Man was stuffed in the bow, hatch-closed, cut off, alone in his steel cocoon, surrounded by dials, gears and bug-eyed periscopes. There was no company for the driver, just the sterile crackle of the intercom as he sat in his small seat, waiting to ride over the unswept road ahead. If there were no mines, if there were no enemy anti-tank rockets, or if there were, if they would miss, then he, invisible in his seat, would be the first into the trees. *How strange to go into battle sitting down,* thought Christopher.

Is there really an enemy on the other side of this paddy? he wondered. *You know there is, over there, waiting for the Americans to come, as they know we must, patiently waiting with machine guns and RPG rockets brought through the harbor they won't let us blockade and down the trails they want us to stop bombing. Bright, shiny bullets, the best the Russians can provide, just waiting on the other side of this little patch of ground.*

Crazy, that's what it is, absolutely insane, said Christopher as he traversed the turret, sweeping with his gunsight trying to see through the drifting white phosphorous cloud.

"Anything stirring, Lieutenant?" asked Burgey, his voice taut over the intercom.

"Nothing, just Willy Peter. The mortars must be keeping their heads down."

"I hope so," spoke up Harris. "I sure as hell hope so."

"Maybe they've split, Lieutenant; maybe they've trucked on back to Hanoi," said Burgey, still looking through his gunsight.

Christopher traversed the turret again, slowly observing the objective, gracefully sweeping the big gun back and forth.

"Those little motherfuckers gonna put some heat on our ass," mumbled Harris, stirring on his seat. "They ain't gone nowhere."

"We'll be moving out soon; let's hold down the chatter,' said Christopher, straining to see again.

The infantry line was almost to the paddy dike intersecting the middle of the field. It was, in turn, split by the muddy road severing the First Squad on the right from the Second and Third on the left.

"Amazing," Christopher whispered to himself as he watched the green line advance at a trot. They were on-line, like soldiers of old, nearly shoulder to shoulder, about five yards abreast, as they charged toward the first paddy dike under the cover of smoke and mortar fire. It was a slightly wavering, serpentine line that slogged quickly through the water and mud, yelling and now firing their weapons in controlled bursts.

The mortar fire intensified upon Malone's radio command, and Christopher could see the orange flashes exploding through the choke of smoke and white phosphorous. He heard the unmistakable sound of shrapnel sing through the air as the mortars splintered in the foliage and trees. Hot Tamale continued to put out a steady barrage of grenade fire.

Sergeant Bush was ahead of the First Squad on the right, and Malone was directly behind Second and Third with Thompson, who had attempted to disguise his radio by bending the antenna downward, tying it to his belt.

All they need are fife and drums, thought Christopher. *Someday in every Southern boy's life. . .bullshit, like Suzie said.*

"'Bout time, huh, Lieutenant?" asked Harris.

"Yeah, when they get to that dike in the middle, halfway across."

"'Bout there, huh," Tripper Man said nervously as he revved up the diesel engine.

"Right."

"War is our business, right, Lieutenant?" cracked Burgey.

"Yeah, and business is good, man, real good," said Tripper Man mashing down the accelerator again, then letting it up.

The engine belched smoke as Tripper Man kept revving the diesel up and up like a horse pawing the ground in anticipation. Sergeant Love's tank revved back.

"Just a routine sweep," somebody mumbled, "just routine."

"Firing switches on," said Christopher.

"Luke the Gook."

"Switches on," answered Burgey.

"Load Cannister when we pass the paddy dike."

"Right," acknowledged Harris.

"I'll give the word," said Christopher, closing his hatch and locking them inside the turret.

"Right," mumbled Harris.

"Half-load the .30."

".30 half-loaded, sir."

"Get some."

"Right!"

"Get some for momma."

"Right."

"Do it for your sweethearts, boys; do it for the Corps."

Sweat dripped into Christopher's eyes, burning them as he looked through the sight to see the Marines reach the paddy dike ahead. There still was no fire from the trees. The platoon lay prone, firing over the top of the levy at unknown targets. They were halfway across. Christopher could see Andy Malone glance over his shoulder at him and reach for the radio receiver from Thompson.

"Go, Chris, go!" was all he said.

"Move, it, go, go, go, go, go!" yelled Christopher over the net to Love and Tripper Man who slipped the tank into gear.

The *Iron Butterfly* jerked forward as Tripper Man pressed the accelerator to the floor. Sergeant Love followed closely behind as they drove a few yards through the brush that paralleled the hamlet, turned left down the muddy road, and plunged into the open for the dash across the field.

Lying behind the levee, Malone watched as Christopher's tanks rolled through the brush and turned left toward them. They reminded him of rogue elephants fleeing from a ravaged village. He wondered if the Vietnamese in the tree line felt like White Hunters as they gripped their RPGs.

"Beautiful, ain't it, Lieutenant?" yelled Thompson, crouching beside him as he tried to be heard over the steady rifle and machine gun fire. Another of Hot Tamale's bloopers thudded into the trees and another mortar round thumped into the mud and foliage behind it, bursting in two quick, almost simultaneous explosions.

"Damn beautiful," Malone yelled back as the tanks drew quickly parallel to them, charging full speed and covering the short distance in a few quick seconds.

"No way they can stop us now, Lieutenant," Thompson replied excitedly.

It was 0751 in the Republic of South Vietnam as Christopher Shaw was racing across one hundred and fifty yards of open rice paddy.

"Roll-mother-fuckers-roll," someone yelled down the line. "Eat 'em up."

"Hurry, Tripper Man, hurry; the quicker the better."

"Hurry, hurry, Barrel; we must get ready for dinner," said Elizabeth.

"Hurry, Chris, hurry," thought Malone. "Luke the Gook."

"What's taking them so damn long?" complained Zell. "Haven't they started? We've got to get that blocking force into position, Major, and quick."

"Barrel, light the candles; we must get the candles lighted."

"Electric switch is on, sir."

"Load Cannister."

"Burn up Charlie's ass. Get some."

Christopher glanced through his bullet-proof glass at the Marines crouched behind the levy, then traversed the turret slightly to the left. The dike and Marines disappeared behind. Sergeant Love traversed to the right. A red flare rocketed into the air overhead and arched gracefully downward. The mortar fire suddenly stopped as the muddy green line stood up from behind the dike and began its assault into the tree line, now running and firing and yelling through the water and mud.

Christopher's tank was almost to the trees, well ahead of the advancing infantry.

"Fire the .30!" he yelled over the intercom above the rocking and roaring of the lunging tank.

"Heat, motherfuckers, heat!" screamed Tripper Man. "Put on the heat!"

The machine gun spit out about ten rounds when a blue and red flash suddenly blinded Christopher, and a fist hit him in the chest.

Andy Malone, running through the mud, looked up in time to see an explosion under the *Iron Butterfly*. The tank lurched dizzily to the right like a wounded animal and plunged off the road into the paddy. Metal parts and track began raining down into the water all around. *Hair* slowed down, paused briefly and churned around its smoking companion. Malone's ears rang as Love began to fire his cannon again and again into the bush, inching forward improving his accruacy.

AK rifle flashes popped from the vegetation as Thompson fell face down, his steel helmet falling off with a dull thud. The green line wavered. Another Marine dropped to Malone's right, and an anti-tank grenade glanced off of Sergeant Love's turret, exploding on the road. Now, in the trees, Love fired cannon and machine gun wildly, turning hard to the left and speeding up, grinding through the thick brush like a mad, steel, green beast. Mortars began to drop into the village and paddy behind. Mud, steel, and smoke mingled together as the line of men lurched forward, staggering and screaming into the trees, firing and reloading without stop.

"Forward, forward!" screamed Malone, but nobody heard. Like one vast green, cresting wave, the platoon hesitated for an instant and crashed down among the trees and vegetation, swirling in the undergrowth, looking for someone to kill. There was no control now as the men fought on their own, tree-to-tree, trench-to-trench, on their bellies, on their feet, yelling, shooting, and crying.

"Keep moving, keep moving," raged Malone again to no one.

Another explosion fell behind Malone, causing him to stagger, and drop to his knees as something burned his back and legs. He fell forward, struggling to keep his face out of the water, only ten yards ahead of his dying radio operator, lying motionless.

"Barrel, where is the wine?" asked Elizabeth as the mine went off under Christopher's tank.

160

Andy Malone tried to crawl forward through the shallow water.

"What the hell is happening at Nam O, Major?" yelled Zell.

"They have established contact, sir," said Craig. "The village reports incoming mortar fire."

"Now we're getting somewhere, Major. Keep em moving; keep em moving; don't let em get bogged down just because they've met a little resistance; keep em moving. They've got to get across."

"Yes, sir."

"Goddamn, goddamn," moaned Tripper Man. "Fucking mine."

"We've lost the right track. Stay inside, stay inside; don't try to get out," ordered Christopher, vomiting on the turret wall.

A bush stood up to the right of Sergeant Love's tank as it swerved through the undergrowth. Christopher, recovering, quickly gripped the turret control, traversed in the direction of the moving bush and pressed the red firing button. *The Iron Butterfly* rocked, and the bush disappeared into mud and blood.

"Fucker had an RPG!" yelled Burgey.

"Shoot, shoot the .30!"

"Fucker had a fucking RPG!" yelled Burgey again.

Burgey put his eyes to his gunsight and began to spray the undergrowth near Sergeant Love. As the Marines swarmed into the vegetation, Christopher's tank fell silent.

The firing stopped, spasmodically at first, then tapering off and finally quitting. Marines wandered about in a daze.

"Sergeant Love, Shaw here."

"Yes, Lieutenant. You all right?"

"Think so, hit a mine, lost the right track. The *Butterfly* is crippled."

"Lucky sir. Gooks bugged out. The grunts are mopping up the shit and blood."

"Good. We're okay, seems like."

"Lieutenant Malone was hit, Lieutenant."

"How bad?"

"Well, mortar. Chest and legs I heard. I don't know for sure."

"We're gonna unbutton and catch up."

"Looks safe."

Christopher and his crew crawled out of the *Butterfly* and sprinted for the nearby trees. Tripper Man opened his hatch, slid down the slope plate and fell to his knees in the mud and paddy water.

"Tripper Man!" Burgey yelled.

Christopher, Burgey and Harris turned and ran back to him.

"Got to carry him," said Harris as the three picked him up and stumbled into the foliage.

"Hey, Doc!" called out a grunt lying in the weeds behind a log. "Tanker needs a fix."

"He'll be number one after this," said the Corpsman coming over giving Tripper Man a shot of morphine. "Just got his bell rung is all."

"No sweat, Lieutenant," Tripper Man smiled looking up at Christopher with blood oozing out of each of his ears. "I be laying pipe in Bangkok fo' long."

"What's up, Chris?" Malone yelled as he sat propped up by a tree.

"Mine blew off the right track is all. Everybody is okay. Driver got a concussion, but Doc says he'll be all right."

"Glad to see you guys could get out of there. Looked bad, man. I was afraid that it punched through; just the track though?"

"Right," said Christopher, going over.

Chrisotopher lighted a cigarette and then another from its end and handed it to his friend with trembling fingers.

"Thompson got blown away," Malone said exhaling smoke and looking at the body covered in a muddy poncho.

"Sorry, Andy."

"Guess we were lucky. No other way across that fucking paddy. Need to get up to Falcon."

"Little bastards were dug in here, real patient like."

"Yeah, looks like a reinforced squad all ready and waiting. They knew we had to come across to get to Falcon, little shits," he said glancing at four Vietnamese bodies that had been lumped together, all staring blankly with dark yellow faces, except for one that was pulpy red. A private walked over and put an unlighted cigarette between the lips of Corporal Nguyen Van Tien; dark blood oozed from his nose, wetting the Winston on the filter.

"He had the RPG," someone said.

"Yeah, and a good pair of binoculars, man, good souvenir."

"No shit? Well, those were made in the U.S.A."

"Hey, gook, want a smoke?" laughed the Marine. "Hey, Hot Tamale, got some tacos for this motherfucker? He says he would like to smoke and eat some tacos."

"Hot Tamale has done sold his peppers, man," someone yelled.

"Looks like he done sold em to these gooks."

"Hot Tamale put boo-coo red peppers in this here tree line, huh, gook," said the Marine walking off, leaving the cigarette dangling from Nguyen's lips.

"Where was that mortar?" asked Christopher.

"Back a ways. They left their baseplate when they split. I think that we may have gotten a couple more, found some drag marks."

"Good."

"You did a job on that one with the RPG. Good shot, I thought he was going to blow Love away."

"Love did great; I'm going to write em up."

"Fine. He saved some lives. He really raised hell in here."

"How do you feel?"

"Okay. Caught some shrapnel in the legs and a little in the back, but I'll skate through. I'll be sitting in Subic Bay soon, chasing round-eyed nurses," he said squirming with pain.

"Lieutenant, got Herman-the-German on the horn; he wants to talk to you, sir," interrupted the new radio operator crouching nearby.

"Tell him all secure, moving out to Falcon. One KIA, three WIA's including me, two priority, one tank out, and four dead gooks confirmed. Medevacs to go out Falcon later."

"Right."

"Do we have contact still with Stubmeyer in the ville?"

"Yes, sir."

"Tell 'em Lieutenant Shaw is the skipper now and will be taking the platoon on up to Falcon. We'll be here with a radio. Tell 'em to send a fire team over from the CAC unit as security."

"Right, sir. We'll head 'em off at the pass."

"What the hell, it's for the freedom loving people of South Vietnam."

"Whatever happened to that old college deferment? I guess we should have gone to graduate school or something and skated, huh, Andy?"

"No shit, I bet Thompson's wondering the same thing. That'll teach him not to go to college with the rich kids."

"No ticker tape this time."

"No, but I'm writing him up, too. Silver Star. I want his folks to feel that it was worth something. Not just the purple heart and knock on the door. He was okay, Chris."

"They'll never understand that. All they'll know is he's dead."

"Maybe."

"Nobody back in the World will ever understand."

"He's ours; they can't claim him, Chris, The World, I mean; really, he's ours." He took a deep drag and flipped the cigarette into an empty foxhole dug by the North Vietnamese.

"Keep 'em spread out, Chris, or they'll get salty and bunch up; you know how they are. Never let 'em bunch up. Remember Boswell. Keep 'em on-line and take it slow. No doubt there'll be booby-traps maybe, and snipers. Take it easy, stay on the horn, and I'll push your communicaton back to those idiots at Battalion, okay?"

"You bet. I'll get a medevac into Falcon as soon as we get there. We'll have you out real fast. You'll be in Subic in a week; won't believe you've ever seen this place."

"Get the blocking force set up; we'll tie in back here. Horrible Hog will be along soon."

"Right."

"Mission first, remember?"

"I seem to remember it being mentioned somewhere."

"Good luck. Keep spread out, man."

"No sweat."

They shook hands, and Christopher turned and walked away, leaving his companion sitting in the mud next to the covered corpse of his radio operator.

The platoon reformed for the final sweep to Falcon. Slowly they trudged behind Sergeant Love's tank as it crawled ahead and emerged from the thick bush of the tree line into the tall elephant grass of the valley that lay at the base of Falcon.

Christopher walked in the middle of the platoon with Burgey and Harris at his side. It was quiet, except for the distant rumble of artillery fire and the low groan of Sergeant Love's tank. It was 0821 in the Republic of South Vietnam as the platoon felt its way cautiously along. Christopher could see Falcon now directly ahead. It was nothing more than a mound of muddy earth that sprung up from the valley floor. It was dirty brown on top with silver barbed wire twisting circles around bunkers that winked out grotesquely like squatting crabs. The link-up was complete.

"What gives at Falcon?" asked Zell.

"They report the platoon in sight, sir, moving up the valley," Craig said opening another Coca Cola can.

"About time," said Zell, *while the guests gathered around the dinner table at the Shaw's party, and Elizabeth's eyes met Conrad's.*

Christopher glanced at his watch; it was 0830. *Quentin broke his watch,* intruded into his mind again. He was frightened that the nausea would return.

A shock ripped through his body before the thought could repeat itself and Elizabeth could pour the red wine. *Mine.* There was a flash. Smoke. He fell backward down in the grass — tall grass, with a funny smell, fresh and wet. *Barrel is here; no, it's Harris, of course, Harris, and now Burgey, too. Okay.*

"I'm okay."

"Corpsman up!"

"Goddamn it, get the doc!"

"Doc! Doc!"

"Over here!"

Doc here, too. Shot. I'm okay, sure thing, gonna pull through. Okay. Get me a chopper.

"Chopper!"

Blood has a peculiar smell. Blood. Boswell. Just like Boswell. Harris please get me a chopper out of Falcon for Christ sakes.

"Chopper soon, Lieutenant. You're all right. Rest easy, sir, everything is gonna be all right now. Chopper is on the way.

"Thanks, Harris."

I'm okay, no sweat, chopper soon, just like Boswell, ". . .in the valley, good farm country." Dull pain. *I'm gonna be okay, not like Boswell.*

"Somebody get on the goddamn horn to Malone!"

"Rifle fire!"

"Gooks! Gooks!"

Shooting has stopped, must have been a sniper. Gooks everywhere. Fuckinggoddamngooks. Somebody kill those fuckinggoddamngooks! Barrel here, no, Harris.

"I'll hang on, sure, thanks."

"You'll skate, Lieutenant. Hang on, man, just hang on, we'll get you out. The chopper's coming."

Doc doing something again. Legs. I need out. I need home, I need to get back. I need to spend some time there. Getting short, real short, not much time left here now. Dad needs me. Mom does, too. I need to be there.

"Hang on, sir."

Sure, chopper's coming. Freedom Bird on the way. No sweat, no fucking sweat. Not long now. Got to get home and help Dad and Barrel; they're getting old. Mom. Queeny. Faith. Maybe someday, near the stars.

"Bring up the right, tell Lieutenant Boswell to bring up the right and tighten it up, he's lagging behind my tanks, he needs to get tighter, but don't bunch up."

Goddamn mines are everywhere, trip wire, fucking trip wire.

"Bring up your people, bring them up!"

Got to get to Falcon, can't wait. Go Noi. Arizona. Happy Valley.

"Traverse right! Shoot! Shoot! Burgey, shoot! Hit it, Tripper Man!"

Tripper Man number one. They all are. I love em. Mom. Road not swept.

"Move out, Chris, you're in charge, keep em spread out. Got to get up to Falcon. Spread out, Corporal. Spread out."

"In every Southern boy's life. . ." Bullshit, Suzie. Quentin. I'll go back to school and teach. Like sitting on a mule. Dad needs me. In those trees. "Gentlemen, your objective will be those trees." Jesus. Sweet Jesus. Queeny. "Do it for your sweethearts; do it for the Corps." Fuck a bunch of Majors. Why? What for? Need to get on home. They'll get me out. Barrel won't let me die here. I'll rest now, wake up later at home.

EPILOGUE

ANDY MALONE SAT LIMPLY beside Christopher's body as the helicopter vibrated upward, hovered, turned slightly sideways like a large insect and flew away from Falcon. Next to him lay Thompson, both zippered in body bags.

Malone stared past the door gunner at the ground below. Back at Battalion, it was a bright red pin on a wall map, but here it was a gouge upon the earth, a canker upon the face of Vietnam. He stared at the door gunner, resting with his gloved hands on the machine gun, looking like a space man with his aviation helmet and wires running from the back of his head to someplace in the helicopter. He could not see the man's eyes or face, covered as they were by a tinted glass visor. The gunner was expressionless. "How many times has he loaded body bags like this?" thought Andy as he rested his hand on Christopher. He felt like holding Christopher next to him and comforting him as one might a frightened child, soothing him and carressing him, telling him all the while that there was nothing to fear, that it would be all right, that life made sense, not to despair, that it was all somehow worth it. Instead, he simply rested his hand gently upon the body and stared at the ground.

"Mission accomplished," announced Major Craig as he spoke over the net to Regimental Headquarters. "We suffered only light casualties, and all reports indicate that the blocking force accounted for our success against the enemy," he repeated over the radio as the helicopter squatted down at the hospital pad.

It was 1830 when Major Craig walked up to Lieutenant Malone's bed where he lay staring at the ceiling. Next to him was a boy with tubes running out of his head and arms.

"Hello, Lieutenant."

Malone did not move but slowly shifted his eyes until they fell upon Craig.

"How you feeling, champ?"

"I'm okay."

"The Doc told me just some shrapnel in the back and legs, just be sore a while, huh?"

"Yeah, something like that."

"Lucky, right?"

Malone did not answer.

"Listen, Andy, I'm sorry about Shaw and Thompson," he said shifting his weight. "They're both getting written up. I brought your Purple Heart, and I'm putting you in for a Silver Star, too." He reached in his pocket and pinned the Purple Heart on Malone's pillow.

"I got enough medals, Major."

"Look, Malone, I'm sorry."

"War is our business, right?"

"That's right, better to die with glory, die in the anesthesia of battle; Malone, you're a fine officer; you know somebody has got to pay the price. You should know that by now."

"Hey, Major, answer me one question."

"Yeah?"

"What is it we're buying?"

There was a pause as Major Craig shifted again. The young man with the tubes moaned and Craig cleared his throat.

"Freedom, that's what we're buying, Lieutenant Malone, our freedom."

"Whose freedom? Those jerks back in the World don't give a damn about us; they think we're criminals."

"I know that Lieutenant, but someday they'll appreciate you and Shaw and Thompson and the men like you. Someday they'll understand."

"Hey, Major, do me a big favor, would you?"

"Sure."

"Get me a priest."